D0866693

TENDER
HARVEST

TENDER
HARVEST

•

Kimberly Llewellyn

AVALON BOOKS
NEW YORK

PRINTED IN THE UNITED STATES OF AMERICA
ON ACID-FREE PAPER
BY HADDON CRAFTSMEN, BLOOMSBURG, PENNSYLVANIA

For all God's cranberry growers.

Acknowledgments

I'd like to thank Paul and Marylou Piscitelli for their New England hospitality when giving the grand tour of Onset Bogs. I couldn't have written this book without your insight and knowledge. Also, a big thank you to Denise Miller whose creativity brought a special touch to this story.

Chapter One

Sally Johnson dropped to her knees and tugged at the few cranberry vines that hadn't been crushed into the ground. She plucked the spared berries from their stems and set them to the side. Frustration rushed through her as she paused to hear the faint squeal of dirt bikes off in the distance.

She narrowed her eyes at the tire tracks embedded in the ground. Having the local kids tear up her dry, vine-laden cranberry bogs with their dirt bikes was something she couldn't afford right now. Not if she were to save the family business, Misty Meadows.

With the need to take out her aggressions, she used her hands as a makeshift rake and frantically scooped her hands through the damaged plants. The sharp sting of thorns prickled her skin while she salvaged a few more precious cranberries. She'd only been home in Pequot, Massachusetts for a handful of days, but the future of the bogs looked bleaker than ever. How would she ever flood the dry bogs and wet-harvest the crop on her own? She desperately wished she could

1

have both her parents back. She'd already come to terms with losing her mother to cancer so many years ago. But her father's heart attack had happened so unexpectedly. It was a painfully sudden blow, not only to her, but to the entire town of Pequot.

A large black shadow appeared on the ground beside her, halting her muddled thoughts. She looked up.

"Casso?" she asked.

"You know they have a machine made for gathering cranberries, remember?" he teased. "It's called a Furford Picker. Been around for a few decades now. It's slow, but better than dry-harvesting the crop with your bare hands."

She nodded up at her late father's best friend. The gentle October winds blew through the man's disheveled white hair. Casso had lived in a tiny bog house on this land for a good twenty years. The New England landscape had been a source of inspiration for his articles for magazines like *Field and Stream* and *Reader's Digest*. If anyone missed her dad as much as she, it was Casso.

"I was just inspecting the damages. I don't have the time to cry over a few mashed berries. Or handpick any more salvaged ones, that's for sure."

Sally couldn't help plucking one more unharmed fruit and adding it to the small pile. She set her forlorn gaze on the trampled vines that crept along the soft bedding of sand and peat soil.

Casso frowned at the dirt-bike tracks. "Rotten teens and their Friday afternoon antics."

"It's all right," she answered halfheartedly, wanting to change the subject. "More importantly, how are you feeling today? You were looking a little green around the gills yesterday."

"Oh, feeling better. I must have caught a bug from one of the students on that field trip who came through here on a bog tour the day before."

"I'm not surprised. You gave all those students the entire tour of the bogs yourself. Little kids are notorious for passing on the sniffles. But I'm glad you're better." She noticed his pad of paper and the pen in hand. "So, what are you doing out here? Feeling good enough to write a new nature essay? More literary musings about Emerson? Thoreau?"

Casso's frown stayed put. "Actually, I happened to be up at the main house when you got a call from your lawyer. He wanted to leave a message before he went on vacation this afternoon. I figured you'd want to know right away."

Sally stopped her inspection of the ravaged crop. The way things had been going, the message had to be bad news.

"And?" she prompted.

"The Wall Street whiz kid is on his way here," Casso said, then sighed.

"What?"

A surge of worry shot through Sally. The very idea of the mysterious secret investor coming from New York to Cape Cod set her on edge. She still didn't know why her father had chosen to take on a silent partner prior to his death in the first place. This whiz kid's request to remain anonymous for a little while longer hadn't helped matters, but when the lawyer had explained that the man had been as upset as she over the loss of her father, she'd agreed to his anonymity—at least for a little while.

"Why is this mystery-partner coming here? What does he know about running a cranberry bog?" she cried out. "Even if he was my father's silent partner, he's got to stay just that—silent. He's got to leave managing the bogs to me."

"There's more, Sally. He plans to unload his share of this place and recoup his losses."

Sally's stomach knotted at Casso's words. She could already imagine the consequences of word getting out that part of Misty Meadows would be up for grabs. Bids would be on the table quickly. People all over eastern Massachusetts and the Cape Cod area would clamor to buy up the property. People like her neighbor, John Merchant, the one man in Pequot her father never got along with.

"Dividing up the land and selling off his share of the bogs won't leave enough land for me or anyone to turn a profit. I'll lose this place. I can't have that— not now. I've lost too much as it is."

She peered out at the dry meadows, fearing the loss of the bogs and possibly the loss of her home. At twenty-seven, she'd already lost a marriage and both her parents. Would she ultimately lose all this too?

A generations-old sense of mistrust filled her. She didn't have to remind Casso of the problems her family had endured over the years. Long before she was born, Sally's grandfather had sold out on the family. He had chosen his best friend over them as a partner when he'd first purchased Misty Meadows. His so-called best friend then swindled him out of half of the property. It had taught her father a valuable lesson about trusting no one and having only yourself to rely on. A lesson he'd passed down to her, with the claim that he would never do such a thing to his own family.

But then history repeated itself. Her father had chosen a partner without even telling her; without asking if she'd have any interest in Misty Meadows. And now, she found herself in the very same predicament as the previous generation: she faced losing another half of what was left of the cranberry yards.

Trust, such a noble trait, had only brought heartache to Sally and her family. Whether it was in a partnership with the bogs, or a partnership in life, Sally knew the cost of trusting someone only to be let down. Her ex-husband's clandestine activities had only further driven home the belief that she had no one in her life she could depend on.

"How could my dad's partner do this to me? He doesn't even know me."

"Sally, don't take his business decision personally. Guys like this only know what they see on a spreadsheet, not what it means to love and labor over the land. I guess he believes it won't turn a profit at all and that it's time to bow out. I think he expects you to do the same."

"I can't. I haven't even been home a week." She dropped her gaze to the berries on the ground—the source of her family's livelihood all these years. The fruit had even come to bring an extra-special meaning to the holidays. But the fruit also needed extra-tender loving care right now, something she planned to provide. "I've got to turn things around and make it right. I mean, I just buried my father—" she choked on the words, "it's gonna take some time. Time I should have given these past few years. I gave up everything to come home and save this place. This whiz kid's got to give this place a chance. He's got to give *me* a chance." She hoisted herself off the ground and yanked up the sleeves of her gray sweatshirt.

"Now, don't panic—"

"Panic? Panic? No, I won't panic. But I can't stand by and let him decide the fate of Misty Meadows, now, can I?" she asked, unsure about the legalities of the whole thing. She tried to recall the exact words in her father's will.

"Now hold on. If it weren't for this guy, you wouldn't have had any bogs to come home to. He gave the financial assistance needed to help your father get by."

"Which, by the way, I still don't understand. You know as well as I do that depending on strangers goes against everything my father believed in and everything he taught me. You know what my family's been through. Right back to my great-grandfather, when he bought this place. We only have ourselves to rely on."

"I know. I know—"

"And now look what happens. This guy wants to sell—"

"Your father didn't say much about the circumstances or the partnership, but I do know this kid came through with every dollar he could spare to help your dad through a rough time. I don't know why this man did it, but you got to give him some credit for that."

"I wish I could, but anyone I've ever relied on has used it against me. That's why I have to become an independent grower again. And that means I've got to convince this man to work out an agreement where he can sell his share to me. I'll pay him in installments for the rest of my life if I have to." She desperately tried to think of ways she could buy out this mysterious mogul when her cash flow was nonexistent. Her stomach knotted tightly. "I can't depend on anyone again only to be left empty-handed." The way her grandfather had ended up. The way her father had.

And even the way she had. Her ex-husband had proven to her once and for all that entering into any sort of partnership—including marriage—would only leave a woman financially and emotionally ruined.

"Has it occurred to you that this guy might be your only hope to save the bogs? That is, if you can convince him not to sell?"

She considered Casso's words. Then, she considered the cost to replace the aging, idle harvesting equipment in the barn as well as the numerous broken sprinkler heads throughout the acreage. The meager insurance payout she'd receive wouldn't even begin to cover the problems she faced. Things seemed to break down at an alarming rate, faster than anything she'd ever seen before, even while growing up. Maybe Casso had a point. Maybe this man was her only hope after all. Sally's shoulders slumped. She had to accept Casso's rationale.

"So what do I do?" she asked.

"Hear him out. Let him have his say, and then convince him up and down and sideways that he's wrong. That he shouldn't sell."

Grateful for Casso's support, she asked, "So when is Mr. Wall Street hotshot due?"

That's when Sally noticed a black Land Rover SUV pull up along the cart path between two bogs.

"Never mind," she said, "I think I just got my answer."

Casso looked over his shoulder at the vehicle and then back at Sally. "It's show time. You'll do fine." He patted the top of her head and lumbered off toward his tiny bog house.

Sally glanced down at her dirt-encrusted jeans and worn sneakers. She smoothed her gray sweatshirt and brushed back loose strands of blond hair that had escaped her ponytail. After that, she gave up any more futile attempts at grooming. She would have preferred to be in one of her crisp linen suits for this little confrontation, but she'd already packed away her corporate outfits in the attic of the main house. Since she'd left her job as an appraiser for Amberlea's Auction House in Atlanta, she'd had no need for such formal attire.

She'd managed to graduate high school at seventeen; college by twenty-one. With various coveted internships under her belt, she had leaped right into the workplace and reaped its awards due to her business savvy in the world of antiques. So why did she find it difficult now to face her fate? Why couldn't she make a simple decision about whether or not to march up to this mystery man . . . or let him come to her? As indecision gripped her, she stood motionless and watched the scene unfold before her.

Once the engine of the large vehicle quieted down, the driver's side door opened. Out stepped a pair of long denim-hugged legs finished off with hiking boots. By his legs alone, Sally could tell this whiz kid was no kid at all, but a full grown, filled-out, adult male. He kept his back to her as he closed the door to his vehicle.

She found it hard to ignore how those jeans embraced his body. Despite the rather warm Indian summer weather, he wore a cable knit sweater with the sleeves pushed up to the elbows, accentuating his masculine frame. She quickly noticed how the man's sable hair stood in sharp contrast to his wheat-colored sweater. His hair would have been impeccable if it hadn't been for the playful gusts of the Cape Cod wind that toyed with his short, satiny locks. Unfortunately, she still couldn't get a good look at the man's face.

His broad back faced her as he surveyed the land ravaged by dirt bikes. His head moved slightly, but enough for Sally to notice. Could he be shaking his head in disdain? Disappointment? Did he see the waste of his hard-earned dollars in these torn-up dried bogs? Or did he share her frustration about the careless youths and their damaging dirt-bike rides?

Slowly, the man turned his sharply angled face in her direction. The cool look in his eyes indicated he meant business.

But his eyes also looked oddly familiar.

From where she stood, Sally knew she'd seen those coal-black eyes before. They were older now—and a little world worn. Despite this, a familiar dangerous spark still loomed in them.

Oh, no. Not him. Please. Anyone but him.

A thorny jab caught in Sally's throat. She forced herself to swallow past the barbed pain. The haunting memories she had tried to escape all these years now accosted her in one, heart-rending blow. This wasn't just some Wall Street whiz kid. This was the first man she'd ever loved. The only man she'd ever lost.

This was Taign McClory.

Chapter Two

Seeing Taign McClory again rocked Sally to her core. How could this be? The reckless boy she'd once shared stolen kisses with had somehow turned into a Wall Street hotshot. He was the last man she needed in her life right now.

Yet here he was.

A cluster of memories jumbled in her head at the sight of him. And with the memories came aching, youthful emotions. Her unresolved feelings for Taign were the toughest thing to come back to. Everything she had encountered since coming home was somehow touched by the memory of him.

At nineteen, Taign had been practically lawless, and trouble inevitably found him. But the veil of mischief surrounding him was only one of the many qualities that had drawn her to him. He'd also made her experience love for the first time at the sweet age of seventeen.

It had also been Taign however, who was the one to teach her the painful lesson about broken hearts and broken trust ten years ago—the night he had skipped town. The night of the devastating brushfires. He'd made promises to her that he'd return for her someday. And she'd believed him.

He had never come back.

Sally swallowed back a long-buried ache. An ache she had thought she would never have to endure again. So . . . Taign had kept his word after all. He *had* returned. But his arrival here today wasn't the kind of homecoming she'd dreamed of as a teen. Because of him, she'd learned all too soon how it felt to love and lose someone. His actions had further taught her not to have faith in anyone, not to trust anyone to keep their word. The few subsequent men she'd attempted to rely on in her life had reinforced that lesson. Her father had been right all along: She'd only have herself to depend on, and she'd have to keep that conviction her entire life.

Despite her ramrod-straight posture, Sally's legs grew numb, ready to buckle out from under her. She willed her limbs to stand strong and stopped her hand from covering her mouth. Such a gesture would be a dead giveaway she was not in control of the situation.

After a mental bucking-up, Sally raised her chin and faced Taign straight on. She stood her ground and decided to let him come to her. Not that she had a choice. Not with her feet firmly rooted amid the creeping vines. For now, she'd merely watch his masculine form in awe.

With a long, deliberate stride, Taign hiked down into the dry bog where she stood. He had the same determined gait she remembered. Same sway of the arms. Same burnished, sepia-hued skin that glowed in the golden autumn light.

He stood before her, his angular jaw set. He didn't say a word. Then again, he never had to. He could merely cast a glance her way and her pulse would start pounding. Had nothing changed in the last ten years?

"Been a long time," he finally said. The hard edges to his face softened as he spoke and Sally could finally see through to the old boyish Taign she remembered. "It's good to see you, Sal. Real good," he added.

"Same here," she lied. "So you're the mysterious Wall Street whiz kid, huh?"

He offered a gentle, imperfect grin. "So they say." The tangy scent of his cologne mingled with the fruity-sweet air and wafted her way. She reluctantly relished the unexpected pleasure.

"I must admit, I'm surprised to learn you're a city-dweller," she began. "I figured you'd wind up working for Mother Nature. You know, like a forest ranger, or owner of your own fleet of fishing trawlers, or something. But never a mogul in New York."

"Hey, Wall Street can be a jungle," he said teasingly.

"I hear it can be ruthless, in fact." She tried to bite back her desperation, but he caught on. He nodded and the all-business edge returned to his expression.

"So you know why I'm here."

"Sure. To take away my bogs," she blurted out.

"*Our* bogs, Sally, *our* bogs."

She didn't want to hear those words. She was too busy tamping down ten year's worth of hurt and confusion that she'd successfully kept repressed until now. Whether she liked it or not, he was here, roiling up those past feelings. When she didn't reply, Taign turned his attention to the bogs. He wandered off, deep in thought, following the trail of tire tracks. Sally absently watched him circle around, his head low, his stare focused on the hard grooves ground into the earth.

Backlit by the low sunset, he stopped to survey the green hills nestled against the undulating wall of distant pine trees. Again, he shook his head in a slow, almost saddened manner. The last time she'd seen him shake his head like that, he'd been rejecting her plea not to leave town.

She still remembered the very night he'd turned her down with the vague explanation that he had to get out of town before it was too late. She knew why. It had been the last night of the Cranberry Festival; a small brushfire had broken out and burned out of control. Based on his whereabouts, he knew he would be blamed. They both knew that. Shortly after his departure from town, rumors had flared about how he must have been responsible for the loss of land and vines from the fires. Other rumors grew too, like how he had supposedly asked the Cranberry Festival Queen to run away and elope with him. It had only been one of many. All Sally knew was that he'd left her behind when he left Pequot.

And now he was back to stake a claim on part of her family's land. Hadn't a claim on her heart been enough all those years ago? She vowed not to let his presence get the best of her. She also reasserted her original goal: Save Misty Meadows at all costs.

The dirt-bike tracks eventually led Taign back to her. "I knew things were bad with the bogs and all," he began, "but I never thought I'd see the day—"

"Yeah, it's pretty bad, but it can be turned around," she cut in, not really sure where to go with her argument. "I know it can. Don't take Misty Meadows away from me."

Taign tilted his head quizzically. "I figured you'd put up a fight about this. Question is, why? You've been gone so long, Sal. Is it because you really care? Or do you still bear a grudge over what happened between us and want to give me a hard time?"

"No," she answered, too quickly. "Even if I've been gone, I do care about the berries. And Misty Meadows. I have no grudges toward you."

Taign's stonelike features relaxed. If she hadn't known any better, she would have thought he looked relieved that she didn't harbor resentment toward him. Did she harbor hurt? Yes. But anger? Hostility? A grudge? No.

"It's just business, Sal." He spoke softly, his voice full of apology.

Of course, it is. Just business, as in, not personal, she said to herself. And nothing more. But these thoughts only made her insides ache more.

"It's just that," she began, her strong tone a poor attempt to mask the hurt, "I didn't expect to see you. I couldn't face the thought of some silent partner marching in here, getting rid of the only thing I have left of my parents. I never dreamed it would be you."

"It's out of my control," he offered.

Sally needed to release the ball of frustration and helplessness that was mounting within her. She couldn't face the man who'd broken her heart and now held her future in the palm of his hands. She dropped back to her knees, frantically raking at the vines with her hands. Furiously, she scooped up the good berries and placed them to the side. Anything to avoid his scrutiny. Anything to avoid a discussion of Misty Meadow's bleak future.

"I—I can't talk about this right now. I've got a job to do. Someone's got to harvest the crop." She dug at the ground with her fingers, paying no attention to the relentless needle-sharp pricks of the thorns.

A set of strong hands came to rest on her shoulders. Taign gently drew Sally to her feet. With his hands still gripping her, he looked at her with a concerned expression in his eyes.

"We have to face this, Sally. And torn-up skin on your hands won't help. The problem with the bogs isn't going away. *I'm* not going away. We have to talk."

"What could we possibly talk about? You came here to tell me you want to sell. Well, I want to save this place. I gave up everything in Atlanta to do it . . . my condo, my career, my husband—"

"Husband?" Taign raised an eyebrow.

Sally hesitated at Taign's surprise. "I mean, *ex*-husband, to be specific. Maybe it'll seem more official once I get the divorce papers back from my lawyer."

She hesitated after the words spilled from her lips. The *divorce papers*. She'd inadvertently left them at the lawyer's office in her haste to get packing and head back home. She couldn't help but think her forgetfulness about the paperwork had been an unconscious effort to forget her ex-husband's antics, including gambling away her life savings. The very thought still shook her to the bone.

"My father never told you I got married?"

"No. I had no idea. I did hear you got yourself some lucrative job in the antique appraisals business after college. But whenever I asked Harry about you, he always changed the subject or had to hang up the phone or something."

Sally stood mute. She wondered why her father would keep the news of her marriage from Taign. She also found herself surprised by Taign's reference to her father as Harry. He'd always referred to her dad as Mr. Johnson. And he'd always revered her father, since Harry had been the only employer in town who had shown enough faith in him to hire him. Somewhere along the line, Taign had grown from dutiful employee to full-blown business partner. She'd have to get used to that.

"I guess, as a topic, you were off-limits." Taign interrupted her thoughts. "Then again, Harry and I didn't get to speak too often."

"So, you sent money his way when you knew how risky berry growing is? What you were thinking?"

"You really don't know why, do you?" With his hands still on her shoulders, he gently squeezed for emphasis.

She feared if she opened her mouth, a jumble of nonsensical words would spill out, so she stood silent, still imprisoned in his grip. A grip that burned to the heart. She'd been too busy with her own riotous thoughts to realize the powerful effect he still had on her until now. How did he still manage to sear her with such heat? When she didn't answer him, he let her go and backed away. But her skin, burned by his touch, wouldn't cool so quickly.

"We better get to the main house. We can talk about the bogs there," he said.

"Why can't we talk right here?"

"No. I really need to get you back to the house."

"Please, whatever you need to say, we can hash it out right here."

"That's not a good idea."

"Why? What's so important that we need to go up to the main house?"

"You're bleeding, for starters."

He clutched her wrists. His sturdy grip immediately captured her attention. The earthiness of his dark arms contrasted sharply against the Finnish whiteness of hers. He turned her wrists upward. Plump beads of blood clung to her skin. She blinked at the red droplets as they rolled along her palms and dropped like scarlet tears to the earth.

"Oh," she muttered, "what was I doing?"

"Taking out your frustrations about this whole mess by digging at the thorny vines," Taign answered. "Come on. I'll take you up to the main house."

"I'm all right. It doesn't hurt." She winced from the mounting sting.

"Still, you've got to get something on them. Come on." With Taign's grasp around her wrists, Sally had no choice but to follow him back to his SUV and then to the main house.

Once inside the two-story Cape-Cod-style home, Taign made her wash her hands at the kitchen sink. He grabbed a handful of paper towels from the rack and gently wrapped her hands in them before settling her down at the vintage Formica kitchen table. He positioned himself in the kitchen chair beside her.

Sally sat in quiet surprise while the man went to work tending to her. Gingerly, he patted her skin dry. She recognized the gentle concern in his expression as he moved his gaze from her face to her fingers. She tried to resist his subtle, disarming smile, but it was a meager attempt. Her heart already warmed to the way he doted on her.

His quiet reverie ended all too soon. With his secure grip, he folded the paper towels around her hands once again and rested them on her lap. Then he broke away from her and rose from the table, and a mass of confusion balled up within her. Admittedly, she liked the tender pressure of his hands on hers. But this realization led to nothing but bewilderment. After all, this was Taign McClory. The man who'd come to sell out on her, but then also took care of her wounds. And she'd let him. Her behavior conflicted sharply with her silent vow not to trust a man again.

He crossed the large kitchen and headed straight to the cabinet that held the first-aid kit.

"I can't believe you still know where everything is," she said.

"I can't believe everything is still in its place. This kitchen is like a time capsule."

She assessed the dated Harvest Gold colored appliances and sunny, but worn, yellow wallpaper. She told herself to keep the conversation light.

"I guess this room could use a little update."

"Oh, no. Don't update it. Don't change a thing. Not a thing."

Surprised by his wistful tone, Sally looked over at the man who was tending to her wounds. He had filled out since the last time she'd seen him; his frame was a little thicker, the expanse of his shoulders a little broader, his posture a little taller. But he'd only been nineteen and still on the lean side when she'd seen him last. She'd been barely seventeen. So much time had passed, and now their lives had come full circle.

Once again, she found herself seated in her kitchen with Taign. As if nothing had changed.

But things *had* changed. Taign no longer spent his spare time as an employee of Misty Meadows. He no longer had to deal with the bias of the people in town—or their whispers about him and his outcast dad. He no longer had to pretend he didn't care, or that the ruthless stories and rumors didn't hurt.

Taign turned back around and sat before Sally. He rested the first-aid kit on the table and opened the lid.

"I can't remember how many times I sat where you are while your mom patched me back together. Sometimes from an accident during a harvest, or when I got into that fight. It didn't matter how I got banged up; she'd take care of me anyway."

"I remember." She also remembered the only fight she'd ever seen him in—when some kids were picking on a girl heading home from school, he'd stepped in to stop them. But people never took the time to hear his side of the story.

Taign paused. "I'm sorry they're both gone now. Your parents, I mean. I would have come to their funerals, but I thought it was best to stay away." He pulled out a bottle of antiseptic and a cotton ball and set them aside. He drew back the towels, unveiling her wrists. Much to her dismay, her hands trembled. She convinced herself it was from all that had happened recently—not from Taign's touch.

With meticulous precision, he dabbed the cotton ball on each deep scratch. The sting of the medicine clashed fiercely with the glorious feel of his hands.

"And I'm sorry it has to be the condition of the bogs that brings us together," he added.

"Are you?" she asked in a hushed whisper.

"Yeah, real sorry. I'm glad to see you again. I wish it were under better circumstances."

"My lawyer left the message you want to sell. I understand, honestly I do. I mean, a sale can mean a lot of money for you. Just fill in those big ol' holes out there with a little dirt and you got prime property for a country club." She paused thoughtfully and waited for a reaction, but nothing broke him from his concentration. She tried a different approach. "Taign, I'm broke. If I weren't, I'd buy your share right now. Anything to keep the bogs in one piece." She tried again to read his expression, but he was focused only on her hands.

When he finished, he turned his attention to her. "Like I said, I wish circumstances could be different. This place has always been an upward battle. The dirt-bike tracks out there are just the tip of the iceberg. It's nothing but senseless vandalism. Those kids have no right destroying other people's property."

"People in town said you did the same thing the night you left," she replied with uncertainty.

"Did they?"

"They said you did a lot of things," she added.

"That doesn't mean they were all true," he countered.

"Probably not."

He packed up the first-aid kit. "I knew what people said back then. Most of the rumors got back to me." He rose, stopped to gaze at the bogs through the large bay window over the kitchen sink, then returned the kit to its rightful place in the cabinet. "But most rumors turn out to be lies."

Sally couldn't help her curiosity about those rumors. Stories of how Taign ruined people's property—Misty

Meadows included—and dodged the police the night of the brushfires. Deep in her heart, she didn't want to believe the stories. They simply couldn't have been true. The families in town were merely looking for a scapegoat. They needed to blame someone for damages to the many local bogs owned by families in the vicinity. Taign seemed like the perfect person, so the rumors had started.

But one particular rumor also gnawed at Sally; the one about Taign and the Cranberry Queen. Yes, rumor had it that he'd asked her to elope with him, and she'd refused. But exactly what words had been exchanged between them before Taign had skipped town late that night? Sally only knew one hard-and-fast truth about the evening: She'd unsuccessfully tried to get Taign to stay in Pequot. When he rejected her plea, he rejected her. The memory made her cheeks burn as scarlet as the cranberries out in the bogs.

She pushed away the desire to ask him about the Cranberry Queen. She thought it best to stick to the topic at hand: the night the town's bogs were destroyed. The same night that Taign had left town.

"Whatever happened is in the past. What's done is done," she asserted, trying to believe the rumors no longer affected her.

Taign quietly closed the cabinet. He kept his back to her as he gripped the counter. Sally stilled, aware she'd ventured onto shaky ground. She couldn't tell whether she'd angered him or conjured up painful memories for him as well. Her heart skipped a beat.

After a moment, he turned and walked toward her. His expression offered no clue to the emotions he harbored. He held one of her hands and inspected his handiwork.

"Like I said, most rumors are lies." He kept his voice low. "No matter what you think happened. Or about anything I may have done that night." He lessened his grip, and she slipped her hand out of his.

"All I'm saying—" she began.

"And all *I'm* saying is don't believe everything you hear. Especially stories about what I did one night ten years ago."

She thought she could detect a hurt mixed with anger. She dropped her gaze to avoid his stare. Her eyes settled on his sweater, on a stain of blood. *Her* blood.

"I'm so sorry—look what I've done. That'll set if I don't get that out for you now." She reached for him—her fingertips barely brushing him—but he lurched back.

"Don't worry about it. It's fine." His eyes wide, a startled look crossed his face. It was the first readable expression she'd seen since he arrived.

"But I can undo what's been done. Let me help you. Let me just work on it." Again, she reached for him, but he stumbled back to keep his distance from her.

"I—I've got some papers out in the car. I meant to bring them in," Taign said. He backed away until he tumbled into a chair. Quickly, he caught the toppling chair and regained his balance—and, for the moment, his composure. He eased the chair back under the table. "I'll be right back." With sudden haste, he spun around and pushed through the screened kitchen door.

Sally slumped back into her seat. What had she done to make him suddenly recoil from her very touch?

You fool. You fool. You fool.

After his mental whipping, Taign climbed down the

patio stairs on the side of the house and stalked over to his vehicle. What had happened to him back there?

He'd lost his cool. That's what had happened. Something inside had snapped and turned him into a bumbling idiot. All because Sally had reached for him. Something he'd dreamed about for ten long years. But not like this. Not under these circumstances. He should have simply broken the bad news about selling and gotten out of there. Before his heart started getting soft. But instead, he'd nursed Sally's wounds. Wounds she'd inflicted on herself because she was going to lose Misty Meadows. And she was going to lose it because of *him*.

He'd done his best to help her dad save Misty Meadows. Long ago, Harry Johnson had believed in him during a time when no one else had. It was only right to help save the bogs. Fat lotta' good it did him. Just as Harry made a dent in turning the place around, the only mentor Taign had ever known passed away. And now, everything at Misty Meadows seemed to be breaking at once, according to recent reports. Right at harvest time too. Murphy's Law, he surmised, even if the damages all looked slightly suspicious to him. Unfortunately, the onslaught of problems had set the place back at square one. His investment in the bogs left him with nothing but empty pockets, and facing his demons.

Taign had learned the hard way not to let raw emotion interfere with net gains and losses. So what made his insides crumble now?

Sally Johnson. That's what. Sally and her ocean-blue eyes and coral-pink lips. Not to mention her long ponytail of tawny blond hair, the color of sun-bleached sand along the Cape Cod shoreline.

Taign opened the door to his SUV and retrieved a small folder with the label *Misty Meadows* typed on the tab. How did this cranberry bog always manage to bring him back to Sally? Maybe the bogs would always be in his blood, the way they were in hers. Speaking of blood, he tugged at his sweater to inspect the bright crimson stain. Sally's blood. On him. Now.

Maybe if he hadn't touched her, he would have been okay. And maybe if she hadn't blushed so sweetly every time he neared her, he could have kept an emotional distance. He chastised himself for not giving her the cold hard facts and getting out of there. He turned and closed the vehicle door, the way he should have closed his heart to her a long time ago . . . but never did.

Before trekking back to the main house, he paused and observed the land once more. Heavy shadows from the distant trees crept and stretched across the ruby-mottled ground, the same way they had for a hundred years. Despite the devastating dirt-bike tracks, he saw only the beauty of the land. He also saw broken dreams.

He'd spent a lot of time out there, and he'd learned everything he could about the earth. As a teen, he'd hoped to one day nurture his own land. But his hopes and dreams had vanished that last fateful night he'd been accused of destroying a number of family-owned bogs, which included the very bogs he'd learned to love the most.

The people of the town believed he'd single-handedly set those runaway brushfires, and he had no choice but to let them believe it. He hadn't been able to think of a better way to protect all parties involved, especially Sally. Soon after, he had needed to get out of Pequot, to break away from his own dad's abusive hand. If he hadn't, he would have wound up like his old man, an angry outcast from this tiny, tight-knit community.

He had dreamed about returning one day as the kind of man Sally deserved to have. He couldn't have achieved any measure of success if he'd stayed in Pequot, Massachusetts. Not with his father sabotaging his efforts. And not with his own reputation as the young rebel who would one day turn out like his old man: dependent on alcohol, alienated, holed out in a weather-beaten sea shack by the docks. With the sole purpose to give grief to the town. But his old man wasn't around anymore to hurt him or anyone else. Taign couldn't decide whether or not to visit the man's grave while in town.

When he looked up at the main house, his thoughts turned back to Sally. No wonder she visibly shook when she saw him. No wonder she looked at him with such hurt in her expression. After all, he had been the town troublemaker who allegedly destroyed part of her father's land so long ago; the rough kid accused of using Harry Johnson's daughter to get a shot at the land through marriage one day.

He'd never meant to hurt her when he left. Never. And yet, here he stood, hurting her all over again with his plans to sell out. He looked down at the manila folder pressed against his blood-stained sweater and thought about the impending sale.

No.

He couldn't do it. Not to her. He wouldn't go through with it.

Heck, he'd unconsciously decided that on the drive down the Cape. He'd told himself he had wanted to sell. He needed to sell. True enough. But not for the petty financial excuses he'd come up with. For personal reasons. To be rid of his past forever. After all, the relentless problems with Misty Meadows had told him that nothing had changed in Pequot and nothing ever would. He'd also told himself that seeing Sally would have no effect on him. None whatsoever.

Well, he'd been wrong.

He no longer cared what the people in the town thought. Didn't care about the old rumors. The suspicions. The stories. The lies. Maybe not much had changed in Pequot, but he'd certainly changed.

And right now, he only cared about Sally and the bogs, he realized. If only he could convince her how he truly cared. With renewed vigor, Taign marched back up to the main house. He entered the kitchen and happily tossed the folder down on the table.

"Sal? Where are you? I need to talk to you! Sal?"

Sally appeared in the kitchen, both hands now wrapped in gauze. "I'm right here. What is it?" She lowered her eyes to the file on the table. "Oh." The disappointment on her face nearly broke him in two. Apparently, the cranberry bogs meant more to her than he had ever realized.

"No, no. It's not what you think. I need you to listen for a minute. I want to help save Misty Meadows." A protective instinct took over and he liked it. This time, he would make things right between them.

Sally looked stunned, her gauze-wrapped hands hung limp by her sides. Then the disappointment in her eyes gave way to bafflement. "You want to *what?*"

"Save Misty Meadows." She offered him no reaction to the good news. "Isn't that what you want?" he pressed her.

Ever so slightly, as though afraid to believe him, Sally nodded.

"So that's what I'm proposing. I'm here to help you. Those bogs are anemic. The bed damages are obvious; it makes the place almost worthless. But we'll make it right. Together we'll make it like it used to be. Just like your father wanted."

Sally stepped back from him. "*We* will make it right? As in, *you and me? Together?*"

"Right. And I'll do everything I can to see it happen, even if I have to stick to you like glue."

"Glue?"

"I'll work beside you twenty-four hours a day. Seven days a week. Whatever it takes."

"I don't know. I mean. . . ."

He understood she'd need a few moments for the information to sink in. To emphasize his point, he stepped toward her. "At least know you can *depend* on me."

That's when her pink lips quavered in response to his offer. To be followed with joyous tears, he was sure.

"So? What do you think?" he asked, ready for the onslaught of those happy, grateful tears on her lovely face.

Her lips parted. Sally sucked in a mouthful of air, which made her chest swell noticeably, even under her gray sweatshirt. She raised her chin as a solitary tear trickled from her eye.

"After ten years," she started to say quietly, then swallowed. "How could you suggest such a thing?"

Chapter Three

Just moments ago, Sally had looked so vulnerable. The kind of vulnerable where he'd wanted to tuck her under his arm and nestle her close. The kind of vulnerable where he was more than happy to comfort her.

But now, Sally stood adorably defiant, her response baffling as all get-out. She shifted on one leg, and her determined little gauze-wrapped fists rested firmly on the soft curve of her hips. When had she sprouted hips anyway?

"You? Stuck to me like glue? I mean, I—I appreciate the offer, but, I can't accept. Not after what I've been through. I just can't."

Confusion tore through him. Was it something he'd said? It couldn't be. He was the answer to her prayers . . . wasn't he? Then again, he might have done the offering, but she'd never asked for his help. Never asked him to show up in the first place.

"Didn't you tell me you wanted to save the bogs and keep your home?"

But she only stared at him all wide eyed. He'd seen

that look before. She'd given him the same look the night he refused her pleas for him to stay and clear his name. He knew the look well, since it had burned itself into his memory after he'd told her how nothing could make him stay. As if he'd had a choice; given the situation.

A knock on the kitchen door, followed with it flying open, broke their visual tug-of-war. Taign turned to see a petite young woman burst into the kitchen, oblivious to the tension inside.

"Let's go! Friday night is pizza night!" the young woman sang out. She stopped abruptly. She exchanged glances with Taign, then pushed back her cropped curly auburn locks to get a better look. "Am I seeing what I'm seeing? I mean, like, is this a dream or something?"

"No, Faith, you're not dreaming," Sally said in resignation.

Taign nailed on his best smile. Another blast from the past. "Hi, Faith."

She gave Taign a bear hug. "I almost didn't recognize you without your long hair and leather jacket. You look so spiffy."

"Things change, I suppose. Glad to see you."

"Ditto. We really miss having you around here. The town of Pequot has been way too . . . quiet. So, what's going on? What are you doing here?" she asked, her grin wide.

"I'm here to help out with wet-harvesting the crop next week, you know, flooding the bogs and all."

"Now hold on," Sally cut in. "I didn't agree to your plan." She crossed her arms, her lips in a full-blown pout.

"It's just like old times seeing you two in here,

head-butting about something." Faith chuckled in delight.

Sally should have known her friend would love this. Always the matchmaker, Faith fully enjoyed witnessing sparks fly between two people. In fact, she ate it up. Sally could already see the gears churning in that well-intentioned, troublemaking, plotting, scheming mind of hers.

"Faith," Sally began, "you said something about pizza?"

"Oh, right! Pequot Pizzeria fills up fast if we don't get in there by six."

"We're kind of in the middle of something here. I don't think—"

"Like I said, just like old times. Hey! Taign, you come, too. Then, you guys can finish your fight—er— chat—there," Faith pulled on Sally's and Taign's arms to prod them both out the door.

"Faith!" Sally blurted out.

Faith halted and let them go.

"What? We're New Englanders. We're hospitable people, or so I hear. It's how we do things. Besides, I'm starving! And I'd love to hear what he's been up to."

"And I'd love to have their pizza. It's been way too long," Taign said.

Sally understood. Being away for so long, she had more than once found herself craving the hometown pizza, with its own distinct flavor her palate would never forget.

"But—" Sally hesitated. "But—"

"No butts about it. If I don't eat soon, I'll pass out. You know about my sugar. Besides," Faith said as she looked up at Taign, "you still owe me ten bucks, remember? As I recall, you were a little low on cash the last night I saw you. A lot of interest accrues over so many years."

"Do you people forget *anything?*" He laughed and held up his hands in defense.

"No," Faith answered matter-of-factly. "How long has it been anyway?"

"Too long. Tell you what, dinner's on me and we'll call it even," he offered.

"Deal." Faith shook Taign's hand.

Sally relented with a groan. "At least let me change out of these dirt-stained clothes."

As Sally exited, her gauze-bandaged hands caught Faith's attention. She turned and glared up at Taign. "What did you do to her?"

"Me? Nothing. Honest." He felt about as guilty as he ever had at nineteen.

"She's a mess! The dirt stains. The blood. She's a walking disaster area! Or hadn't you noticed?"

"Believe me, I noticed." *That and a whole lot more.*

She stabbed a finger at the bloodstain on his sweater. "And look at you! When you two fight—"

"We weren't fighting."

"Then what's with the lobster claw wrapping on her hands?"

"It's gauze. I caught her dry-harvesting cranberry vines bare-handed."

"What?"

"Taking out her frustration."

"About you?"

"No," he answered, then added, "maybe. I don't know." What was it about this town that kept him on the defensive? "But I do know, some kids on dirt bikes apparently used a bog as a motocross earlier this afternoon. Tore it up pretty bad. Got her awful upset. It's understandable."

"Was it you on one of those dirt bikes?" she taunted.

"I haven't been on a dirt bike in years," he quickly assured her, and recalled how Faith loved to get a rise out of people. But she wouldn't get her way today. "Come on, if you're done with your interrogation, we can wait for Sally outside. I'll drive." He opened the screen door and gestured a "ladies first" with his hand.

Faith gave him the once-over before she walked out the door. "Hmm. So, you're really back, huh? You really gonna help out around here?" she asked Taign.

"Something like that," he answered as he followed her.

"But Sally hasn't agreed?"

"Not yet. Don't worry, she'll come around. She'll see things my way."

Faith belted out a laugh. "If Sally Johnson inherited one trait from her father, it's his stubbornness."

She marched haughtily toward the black SUV. "A Land Rover, huh? You must be doing pretty well for yourself."

"I do all right." Taign unlocked the doors with his remote keyless entry, then opened the back door for her. But she didn't climb in. Instead she stood there, eyeing him, suspicion playing across her cherub-like face.

"I always liked you, Taign. But I'm warning you, don't hurt her."

"You know I never meant to—"

"I'm sure you never *meant* to, but she's been through a lot lately, and she doesn't need anyone— and I mean *anyone*—messing with her right now."

"You mean like her ex-husband?"

Faith nodded. "She took a chance on him and got hurt real bad. She'll never risk that again. 'Course, she has us—her friends. And we all offered to help at harvest time, but she won't have any of it. She wants to pay some people, somehow, so there's no strings attached, or some such nonsense. So, I say to her, 'You know that's not how we do things.' But she still insists on hiring help."

"But that's *not* how it works. Everyone pitches in at harvest."

"Like I said, she got hurt and that's that. And with all the problems going on around here, she just knows there'll be bids on the table for her bogs soon. It happens whenever anyone's bogs get into trouble. She doesn't know who really wants to help and who really wants to buy the place out from under her. She doesn't know who she can trust, so she wants to pay workers and owe no favors to nobody. She believes she has only herself to depend on. End of story."

Taign fell against the vehicle and groaned. "So that explains her reaction earlier."

"What reaction?"

He looked toward the sky. Foolish. He'd been absolutely foolish. "I told her she could *depend* on me. And once I said it, I swear I thought she cracked in two. I couldn't figure out why."

"You've got to admit, your track record with her isn't too great. I don't see any reason why she should believe you."

"I'm here, aren't I?"

Faith belted out another laugh. "Yeah? For how long?"

"As long as it takes." Taign needed to have Faith on his side. Convincing Sally to give him a chance would prove tougher than he'd thought. "Faith, you gotta help me out here."

"What? Me? What can I do?"

"Tell me what happened with her husband."

"It's no secret. Then again, nothing's a secret in this town. The guy seemed so nice, until he gambled away her entire savings, using her the whole time. Sally had intended to put her money into a new home. Not a very nice situation. He had everyone fooled, even Sally."

Taign glanced over Faith's shoulder to see Sally climb down the stairs of her patio and approach them. With her ponytail now gone, her brushed-out tawny hair tumbled freely about her shoulders, much like it had when she was seventeen. The sight of her had the same intoxicating effect on him now as it had back then. No one but Sally could look so lovely in an old pastel blue and pink flannel shirt that hinted of the curves underneath. How had he ever had the strength to say good-bye to her that night? Yes, she'd been so young, with too much world to conquer for him to be messing with her life, but he still didn't know how he'd managed to walk away.

Taign shook off the nagging thought. He'd done the right thing at the time. He'd just have to smother his regret over the decision. He turned back to Faith.

"Here she comes. Thanks for the info."

"Sure. But remember what I said. Not one hair on her head gets hurt, got it?" She hoisted her little body into the backseat of the vehicle.

"You have my word."

He started to shut the door, but Faith stopped him. "Oh, and Taign. . . ." She paused thoughtfully. "Good luck. You're gonna need it."

He nodded a thanks and jogged over to the front passenger side to open Sally's door. But Sally got there first. She climbed in, with barely a glance to him. He looked helplessly at Faith, who offered him a shrug followed by a reassuring thumbs-up.

With a sigh, he trudged over to his own door. It would take more than a simple chivalrous act to sway Sally in his favor.

"McClory! Your table is ready!"

The announcement sent more than a few odd looks their way, Sally noticed. Most people in town still knew the infamous McClory name and she imagined they were probably not too thrilled to hear it, even after all this time. Old scars ran deep around here.

Ignoring their glances, she followed Taign, who eased his way through the crowd of people at the pizza parlor. Faith straggled behind to say hello to a few customers she knew and catch up on the latest town gossip.

Sally hoped the dark atmosphere of the pizzeria would cast them in shadow, and make them barely recognizable. Taign McClory's presence in town could mean trouble, and she was in no mood for an evening brawl.

When she sat down at the booth, Taign slid in next to her and sat a little too close. She hadn't recalled until now how cramped the booths were at the pizzeria. Even so, did Taign have to sit so close? Maybe he couldn't help it if his substantially muscular frame took up the whole booth the way it did. Then again, if she didn't know better, she'd swear he crowded her simply to get a reaction out of her.

If so, he was succeeding. But she couldn't let him

get away with it. No way, no how. She had to demand he move to the seat across from her. Now. Before it was too late. Before she decided she liked him this near.

Just as she opened her mouth to object, Faith claimed the seat across the table. Sally had momentarily lost her opportunity to make him get out and sit opposite her. If she said anything now, it would be clear that he was already getting to her. She willfully controlled the surge of uneasiness within her. After regaining her composure, she mentally prepared herself to endure his invasion of her personal space.

"Mark's supposed to meet up with us," Faith announced.

"Didn't you and Mark break up?" Sally asked. Her voice didn't have to crack like that, now did it? Self-conscious, she cleared her throat. Twice.

"Yeah, we did. But then he showed up at the shop this afternoon and the next thing you know, we're back together." Faith blinked, as though not sure whether to believe it herself.

Sally turned to Taign. "Faith opened up an antiques-and-collectibles shop a few years ago. In the historic district, downtown Pequot." While Sally and Faith shared the same passion for the decorative arts, their passion had led them down two different career paths.

"That's one thing Sally and I both really like—antiques and vintage stuff. I must admit, business has been great," Faith continued. "Too great, I'm afraid. Space is tight in that little shop. There's no more storefront property left to expand. I can't rent any more room even if I wanted to."

"Sounds like a good problem to have," Taign offered.

"Oh, sure. I can't complain. I'm just having some growing pains. I need more elbowroom to refurbish furniture and accessories. You know, like a studio off-site. A place with enough open space and square footage to store the stuff I acquire throughout the year. Tourism on the Cape may be high, but so is rent. I just gotta be careful not expand beyond my means."

"Wise thinking," Taign answered, just as the food server appeared to take their order of sodas and pizza.

An old rock song played on the jukebox in the background. Faith let out a whine. "Won't these people *ever* grow up? Sheesh, this was our prom's theme song. Enough already with the Zeppelin-Van-Skynard stuff." She held an open palm out toward Taign. "Give me some quarters and nobody gets hurt."

As if out of an old habit, Taign dutifully searched his pockets and handed her a fistful of change. When the drinks arrived, Sally noticed Faith's boyfriend over by the pool tables; she could tell it was him by the ponytail at the nape of his neck.

"There's Mark, just starting a game of pool," Sally said before Faith left the booth.

"Mark? Here? Already? Where?" Faith leaned forward to scan the pool table area. "Oh, yeah! I'll see you two when the pizza comes. But first I've got to go pick some tunes from this decade and go see my love." She leaped from the booth, then wavered. She scrutinized Sally's face. "You okay here? You know, alone with him?" She tilted her head toward Taign.

Sally nodded. "I'm a big girl. I'll be okay."

"I'll be right over there if you need me." Faith spun on her heel and darted toward the old-fashioned juke box.

"She's pretty protective of you." Taign took a hard swallow of his drink.

"She's a good friend. Not many people can say they still have their best friend from high school."

"True."

Despite the wail of the jukebox, a silence settled between them. She wanted to screw up the courage again and beg him to move to the other side of the booth, but decided against it. By now, it would be a sure giveaway that he made her crazy inside and she couldn't have that. Instead, she toyed with her frosty glass, trying not to notice how Taign watched her. Slowly, he took one of her hands and inspected the gauze.

After so long, he still had the uncanny ability to turn her into putty. How could this be? In a stupor of confusion, Sally stared blankly down at the bandages on her skin. She knew she should pull away, but her hand had already melded into his.

"I forgot I had this wrapping on. I must look ridiculous," she managed to say. With her other hand, she reached up to tear off the cottony material.

"Here, let me." Slowly, he unraveled the gauze, exposing her raw skin to the air. She bit back a wince, but Taign must have seen her pained expression because he raised her hand and kissed it. Somehow, his kiss took the edge off the sting. He held her other hand and did the same.

With the rest of her ready to melt and ooze onto the seat, Sally once again found herself inundated with old feelings. Feelings of unresolved longing for the one man she'd lost. The kind of feelings she had no business having. Where had they gotten her last time?

"Taign, what are you really doing here?" She

wanted to sound firm. Angry, even. But she only came across sounding like a pathetic teenager in love.

He gave her hand a final kiss and brought it down to the table. "You know why I'm here."

"You came to sell and recoup your losses, as I recall."

He shook his head. "No. I mean, at first, maybe. And yes, I'd like to recoup my losses, but not just with the bog—"

"My father had no right to bring in a silent partner," she said, still confused over the business decision.

The decision didn't make sense, but in reality, she'd had no control over her father's dealings at the time. After all, she'd been the one to turn her back on the land so long ago when she moved to Atlanta. She didn't mean to cause a strain when she left. The time had come to strike out on her own to see what else was out in the world; to pursue one of her other interests—namely, antiques and appraisals.

"Your father had no choice but to approach me—"

"Approach you? How did he ever find you?"

"Let's just say he was the one person I occasionally stayed in contact with over the years."

"I never knew. . . ."

"It took a lot for him to come to me and ask for help. Let's face it, your dad was never the same after your mom died. He told me he felt the bogs slipping through his fingers, and you had no interest in them at the time. He figured I'd do what was best for Misty Meadows."

"Like unloading the place?" She didn't mean to sound so hurt and fearful.

Taign sat quiet for a moment. "I thought selling was the only way. But—"

"But what?"

"But then I saw you literally tear yourself apart, desperately holding on. The bogs are in bad shape. Real bad. Only a couple are worth harvesting this season."

"I know all about it."

"And I know you don't have the means to pay for hired help."

"I'll find a way. I'll have to. I don't know who to trust right now. I don't know who really wants to help and who wants to buy the place out from under me. The equipment alone is breaking worse than I ever saw. I can't let word get out. . . ."

"Hiring others is not how it's done and you know it. This may sound strange coming from me, and I'm sure it's hard to put your faith in the people of Pequot right now, but this town is a community. They pull together at harvest—"

"I know how it's usually done. And I know I sound unreasonable, but I really think it's best for me to apply for a loan and—"

"And put yourself in debt even more? If you get a loan—which I doubt—then you'll never climb out of your financial hole, not as an independent bog owner. Besides, you need more than just money." He captured her gaze with his. "You need *me*."

Taign was the last person she needed, and Sally had already tried to tell him that. Unfortunately, he was too obstinate to listen. She lowered her lids, unable to face his stare.

"You don't understand, Taign. Since I've been on my own, I've learned one thing. I can't afford to depend on others." Her past assaulted her in a flood of memories. Not only memories of her ex-husband, but also memories of Taign's turning away from her. When the pain hit her, she willed herself not to cry. "My *heart* can't afford it," she whispered. She pulled her hands out of his grip once and for all.

She glanced up in time to see the server set their pizza on the table. Mark and Faith joined them. Sally pulled herself together and introduced Mark. To avoid further conversation with Taign, she bit heartily into a slice of pizza. She forced herself not to be a killjoy and tried to have a good time with her friends. After endless moments, however, she realized Faith was unusually silent.

"What's wrong? You're awful quiet," Sally remarked.

"Nothing. Don't worry about it."

"That's exactly why I'm worried. What is it?"

Faith paused, then spoke. "I overhead some of the guys by the pool table—"

"About Taign being here, right?" Sally elbowed him in the side. "Trouble seems to follow you, doesn't it?"

Taign's mouth was full and a drop of oil glistened on his lip, but Sally tried to act like she didn't notice. She reminded herself this was neither the time, nor the place, *nor the man* to think about lips, and kissing them.

Faith shook her head. "They're not mad about Taign. Okay, maybe they're a little mad. But that's not it. They were talking about John Merchant. He plans to try and buy Misty Meadows again."

Sally almost choked on her pizza. Yes, she knew offers to buy the place would pop up on her. But this soon? And from John Merchant of all people? Her father and John hadn't exactly gotten along, to put it kindly. What made John think she would betray her

father and sell to him? He hadn't been the friendliest
of neighbors over the years, although he'd been more
than happy to try and take away her father's bogs on
occasion.

"Won't he ever give up? For goodness sake, he
practically shoved my father into his grave!" She
dropped her pizza slice to the plate. "Even with my
father gone, John wants to out-do him and take over
the property. So what if he owns all the land surrounding me, does that mean he has to own my bogs too?"

She rose and gazed around the pizzeria to see if she
could find John Merchant. She needed to settle this
rivalry between him and her father once and for all.
Misty Meadows was not for sale, and she'd tell him
so.

Taign put his hands around her waist and settled her
back into the booth. Immediately calmed down by his
touch, Sally was surprised by the fact he still had that
kind of power over her.

"Like I said, it'll never happen," she told them
again.

Faith's forehead wrinkled. "But Sally, he says it's
practically a done deal."

"Done deal? My father may not have been great at
business, but he was a good berry grower. The best,
in fact. He loved his bogs. They would have dried up
years ago if it weren't for him. And he'd never sell to
John Merchant. I don't know what John's talking
about." Sally turned to Taign. "Do you know anything
about this?"

Taign hesitated, which was all the answer she
needed. So, Taign had something to do with John Merchant's boasts. Taign had come with plans to sell. John
Merchant had been bragging that the sale of Misty

Meadows was a done deal. The pieces quickly fell into place. Suddenly, she needed to get out of there. It was too much. The stares. The glares. The talk. The threat to her homestead by her father's rival. All the while, Taign had sat beside her, knowing more about her own bog business than she did.

She rose again, wanting to slide out of the booth. "Let me out."

"Come on, Sal, wait a minute. Don't run away. Let me explain—" He didn't budge, didn't let her out. Sally remained trapped inside the booth. But not for long.

"I'm telling you, if you don't move out of my way, I'll climb right over you," she threatened.

"I'd like to see you try—" Still seated, he opened his arms wide, as though more than ready to tangle with her.

"Taign!"

"Okay! Okay! Where are we going?" he asked in acquiescence as he slid out of the booth.

She hopped out of the booth and sidled past him. "You're staying here. I'm going. I need to be alone," she said in as firm a tone as she could muster.

"Alone is the last thing you need to be right now. You're not alone in this, Sal. Not anymore." Taign grabbed her wrist and drew her back toward him. He leaned in so close, his warm breath feathered onto her skin. She needed to resist him, needed to resist his touch, his smile, and his offer of help. Even if he blocked her escape.

"Now you listen to me," she began, "you may own something like half my bog, but you *don't* own me, Taign McClory."

"Oh, Sal," he remarked, almost apologetically, "I own more than that."

His answer took her by surprise. Unsure if he meant her heart or her bogs, she stood there and waited for him to explain.

"I own fifty-*one* percent of Misty Meadows," he confessed.

"What?"

"Your father insisted."

"He wouldn't—"

"He did."

Chapter Four

Stunned by what she'd learned, Sally stood rooted to the floor of the pizzeria. She didn't dare move until she let the sobering words sink in. Could it be? Her father had handed over more than half the property to Taign? Such an action without explanation went against everything her father had taught her about remaining independent at all costs—not to mention not relying on, or trusting, anyone again.

She didn't know who to be more upset with, her father who'd put her in such a position, or Taign who'd come back into her life at the worst possible time. She should have paid more attention to her father's piles of records after his death. But the funeral arrangements, along with the neglected cranberry yards, had kept her away from the mountains of paperwork. Her fight-or-flight response finally left her body.

"Please, I just need to get some air," she murmured, "and collect my thoughts."

Her sudden acquiescence made Taign release her

and allow her to pass. As she left the table, she heard Faith yelling out something. During a break in the music, Sally heard her friend say, "Well, don't just stand there! Do something!"

Sally looked back to see Faith urging Taign to go after her. Even her best friend wouldn't let her be solitary, not for a moment. What was she trying to do? Whose side was she on, anyway? Out of the corner of her eye, she could see Taign dash toward her, but it only made Sally flee the pizzeria faster.

Once she found her way to the pay phone outside, she rummaged through her pockets for change to make a phone call. But her pockets were empty. It didn't help that she'd left her purse back at the table. Before she could figure out what to do next, Taign rounded the corner and filled up the space before her.

"I—um—don't have any change. Do you have any?" she asked him. Hopefully, it wouldn't matter that she'd just run off because of him and he'd give her some change anyway.

"What's with you women and no pocket change? I gave it all to Faith, remember?" He laughed, despite her predicament. How could he see the humor in all this? She picked up the receiver anyway.

"I'll—I'll call collect."

"You'll call who?"

"My lawyer."

"Why?"

"To fire him."

"For what?"

"For keeping me out of the loop."

"He's an old friend of your father's. He wanted to protect you and not bother you just yet with any more problems."

"He shouldn't decide such things. Does *everyone* have to be 'old friends' in this town? Does everyone have to feel the need to protect me? I'm not seventeen anymore. And I'm going to call him and tell him so."

"You think he'll be in the office at seven o'clock on a Friday night?"

"I'll leave a message on his answering machine."

"Then who'll accept the charges?"

Sally let out a groan and hung the receiver back on the hook. As she did, she recalled how her lawyer would be out of town for a few days on vacation as well. Talk about terrible timing.

With Taign a hairbreadth away, she had no time to dwell on the attorney. Caged in by his presence, she made a meager attempt to sidestep him and slink back inside. Again he carefully gripped her arm.

"Oh, no, you don't," he insisted, "you're not going anywhere. Not until we discuss a thing or two. Come on."

He gently tugged her along behind the building, which overlooked a small grassy cove. Nightfall had already settled around them. If it hadn't been for the bright red neon sign on top of the pizzeria, they would have been left in complete darkness.

Sally leaned against the brick building. She didn't bother trying to escape, not when Taign pinned his gaze on her. His stare alone kept her backed against the wall.

"You need to listen to me," he began.

"I'm listening." She clasped her hands together and waited for what he had to say.

"It's true, I got a brief message about some sort of bid on the table right before I came down here. But I didn't know who. I had no details. My business associate must have arranged something without my knowledge. Or John Merchant likes to brag about nothing. He always has."

"So you're in the dark as much as I am?"

"Pretty much. I'll call my associate first thing on Monday to find out what's going on, all right? Nothing can happen without my say-so. I mean, *our* say-so."

Unsure whether or not she felt better, Sally asked, "But why didn't you tell me about the offer?"

"It was a moot point. Like I said, I want to help. I want to give this place one last shot. I'm not here to complicate things."

Complicate things? Did he say, complicate things? Nothing could be more complicated than having this man back in her life, backing her against a wall, telling her he *didn't* come here to complicate things.

"You said you want to give the bog one last shot, but what if we fail?" she asked.

"One crisis at a time, okay? Let's see how harvest goes."

"And if we succeed?"

Confusion flared in his eyes. Obviously, he hadn't thought the situation through; hadn't considered the next step in his scheme if all went according to plan. Taign had yet to mention what he planned to do after the harvest.

He broke from her, apparently stunned he still stood before her, virtually holding her fast against the wall.

"Let's see," he began cautiously. "If we succeed, then you can keep your home and property. And I . . . um. . . ."

"Go back to New York?"

He didn't say anything. Instead, he lowered his gaze to the ground. Despite the harsh light of the neon sign,

Taign looked great, which made the truth all the more difficult. He still had a magical handsomeness that was hard to deny, even if he had driven her up a wall in the short time he'd been home.

Yes, he'd go home, back to New York, she knew.

"Right," he eventually said, "New York."

"Back to where you belong," she added purposefully. Deep down, she knew he had no intentions of staying in the sleepy little town of Pequot. But she wanted to hear it from him.

He rubbed the back of his neck, as if a sudden ache had started there. Stepping back, he gave her room to flee.

She stayed put. She had to get it out in the open and discuss whether or not his business here in Pequot was a temporary gig.

"New York is where you've made a life as a bigshot financial analyst, remember? And once harvest season is done, the hard part is over. Then you can leave."

"I do have to go back sometime, it's true. But right now, I've taken a few weeks off and can stick around for a while. A workaholic like me—with no family—tends to accrue a heck of a lot of vacation time."

"And you've chosen to spend your vacation here?"

"Sure. If it meant I got to see you again."

Sally braced her arms against the brick wall. She needed its support. "What are you saying? After all this time, you wanted to see me? With the way we left things, I figured I'd be the last person you'd want to see."

"Actually, the opposite."

She sank to the ground and sat back against the wall, her heart pounding at his words. She looked down at her hands where Taign had kissed her earlier. She couldn't bear to face him, not after how his honest words pierced her to the soul. He seemed to take aim and fire at will. And he hit his target every time . . . her vulnerable heart.

"I thought you were here on business. Misty Meadows. Nothing more."

"Oh, Sally." Taign knelt beside her and spoke gently. "We always said the bogs brought us together—you and me. Every summer. Every school vacation. Like the time we sanded the dry marshes in the dead of winter." He paused. "And like right now. For the wet harvest coming up."

"No. It wasn't the bogs that brought us together this time. It was my father's death."

"He was part of it. But the bogs were in trouble, and he trusted me. Always had. He never believed the rumors about me, not one."

"I remember. Even when he lost part of Misty Meadows to the brushfires the night you left town, he never questioned you. Somehow, he knew you didn't set those fires."

"I'll never forget how he believed in me."

Sally couldn't miss the regret in his voice. But it only raised the same old questions. "So, why didn't you stay and stand up for yourself to everyone else in town? Why did you leave? It made you look so guilty." Even she couldn't mistake how condemning his action had been. He'd behaved so strangely that night, she still couldn't put the pieces together.

"It was time for me to go. Let's just leave it at that and focus on the here and now." Taign rose and gently pulled Sally up with him.

"You really do want to help, don't you?" she asked, still unsure.

Taign nodded, the red neon light shimmering on his black hair. "Why don't we head back inside before all the pizza's gone?"

"But I have so many more questions." Like the one about him and the Cranberry Queen.

"Enough for one night. We've got plenty of time for answers."

On the drive home, Sally remained quiet while Faith filled Taign in on the soap opera events in Pequot over the past few years. She rattled off the people who'd stayed. People who'd gone off to college. Those who'd enlisted. What jock had married which cheerleader. And how the class valedictorian hadn't been able to hack his first semester at Harvard and wound up as cashier at the local roadside produce stand.

As the van pulled up to the modest two-story house full of so many memories, Sally let out a pent-up sigh. She'd managed to make it through the night with Taign. She'd even survived the weekly Friday-night brawl at the pizzeria . . . a brawl that hadn't included him, much to her surprise.

Faith hopped out of the SUV. She came around and met Sally on the passenger side.

"So, can you still meet me for lunch tomorrow? We can brown bag it and eat down at the pier," she said. "I'd like to run some business ideas by you. Maybe brainstorm what to do about my shop's growth spurt."

"Wouldn't miss it." Sally would need the diversion. Chaos and Taign seemed to go hand in hand.

"Meet me at my shop around noon. Oh, and I set aside the antique linens you liked so much. I know the Saturday afternoon crowd would have pounced on them if I hadn't. You can take them home tomorrow."

Sally brought her hand to heart. She'd loved those linens since the moment she'd noticed them in Faith's little antique and vintage shop. Unfortunately, her eyes were bigger than her purse.

"It's all right. You go on and sell them. I can't afford—"

Faith plugged her tiny fingers in her ears and blocked out Sally's answer by humming off-key. After a few seconds, she pulled her fingers out of her ears.

"I won't hear of it. Not a word. You've wanted those linens for weeks. You pay me when you can. The holidays are right around the corner. They'll look great in your dining room." Faith waved a good-bye and bounded over to her van where Mark waited.

Although her friend had abandoned her, Sally didn't have to look to know Taign still stood achingly near. Her body tingled in his presence. Suddenly, the night had taken on a chill that made Sally shudder. The shuddering *was* from the cool night air, right?

The evening had come to a close, but Sally didn't know what kind of evening it had been. A night out with old friends? With an old first love? Or would she call it an impromptu date with Taign after all? Suddenly feeling awkward, she angled herself toward him.

"I guess this is good night."

Taign smiled. "I guess it is."

She shook his hand, then strode toward the patio steps.

"See you in the morning," he called out.

Sally had only made it up one step before stopping. Did he say, "in the morning?" She turned to see him open the back door to his vehicle. He pulled out a blanket, a large duffel bag, and a hurricane lamp.

"Um, what are you doing?"

He grinned up at her. "Getting ready for bed."

"Where—right here? On the ground?"

"Nope."

She wondered if this was the part where he told her he owned fifty-one percent of the house too. She couldn't stop the uneasiness that pooled within her.

"Then where? In . . . um . . . the main house?" she asked, and mentally prepared herself to go to the nearest hotel or crash at Faith's place, if need be.

"Nope. I won't be sleeping in there."

"Then where are you going to stay?"

"You guys still have seasonal tours for visitors and school field trips, don't you?"

"Yes. . . ."

"And you still have a few historic bog houses as part of the tour? The ones with all the fancy trimmings? Like a cot and a wood stove?"

"Yeah, but—"

"Then you'll know where to find me."

"I can't let you stay in a measly old shack out in the woods."

"Why not? They're fully functional. And the berry pickers used to live in bog houses during harvest. It was done for a hundred years. Casso's lived in a bog house for twenty years."

"Don't let Casso fool you. He may not admit it, but when it gets too rough out, he sneaks up into the main house and sleeps on the couch. Besides, his shack has got more than its share of creature comforts."

"I've got all my creature comforts right in here." He patted his duffel bag.

"You're not serious, are you?" Sally asked.

"Never been more serious in my life."

"So I'm really-truly not getting rid of you anytime soon, am I?"

"Got that right."

"So you're not gonna tell me you own fifty-one percent of my house? 'Cause if you do, then I'm the one who should move into a bog house."

"No. That'll always stay your house. No business deal will change that. I'm staying out here."

Taign lowered his duffel bag to the ground and sauntered over to her. With her still on the bottom step, the added height allowed her to look straight into his eyes.

"Will you be all right?" he asked.

"I'll be fine," she answered, hopeful he didn't catch the quiver in her voice. She had to keep control, even if he stood devastatingly near. If she didn't remain calm, she'd wind up in a whole heap of emotional trouble with this man. She decided to gain the upper hand by saying, "But I'm worried about you roughing it alone in the wild. City life might have made you soft. Are you sure you can handle it?" She couldn't resist the urge to tease him. It had always worked in the past as a means to keep them on even ground.

With a raise of an eyebrow, he pondered her question. "Oh, I can handle it. The real question is, can you?" He kept his steady stare on her. It was the same mischievous gaze he'd always had. Taign still meant trouble, no matter how hard she might try to ignore the fact.

"I'm not afraid of some Wall Street hotshot. I can handle it." Outwardly, she grinned with confidence. But on the inside, well, that was different story.

Okay, maybe I'm a little afraid, she silently admitted. Maybe even downright fearful of how his stare alone made her tingle down to her fingers and toes. But she couldn't let on.

He narrowed the little gap between them, his face cast in half shadow from the dim porch light. "I wish I could be so strong. But I'm not handling seeing you again as well as I'd hoped."

"You're not?" she asked in surprise. His confession caught her off guard.

"No, I'm afraid not." This time he wrapped his hands around her waist and pulled her into him. "In fact, I'm having a heck of a time handling the mixed signals you're sending."

"Me? Sending mixed signals?" After all, with his hands embracing her, wasn't *he* the one sending mixed signals? "I'm doing no such thing."

"Then why am I wanting to pick up right where we left off years ago? It's as if time stood still. As if nothing's changed."

"Time didn't stand still," she answered on a wisp of a breath. "And everything's changed."

Maybe if she convinced him, she could convince herself. Her breaths rose and fell as she tried to calm herself while in this man's hold. But he made it impossible for her. Absolutely. Positively. Impossible. She leaned into him.

"There you go, doing it again," he murmured.

"Doing what?" she asked, filled with a sudden curiosity about what he meant.

"Sending out mixed signals."

"I can assure you, I'm not sending out any mixed signals." Although she tried to deny the charge, she couldn't help feeling dizzy in his presence.

"Yeah? Then why am I about to kiss you?"

Chapter Five

Before Sally had a chance to toss him any sort of witty response, Taign crushed his lips against hers. Silenced by the kiss, she could do nothing but indulge in the sweetness of his mouth. He tasted familiar and yet excitingly new. This was a kiss from a man of the world, not from the boy she remembered.

The heat of his mouth mixed with the woodsy scent of his skin urged her to kiss him back. He tasted of the night, a blend of warmth and musk and danger, which evoked memories of leather jackets and motorcycles. But she could also taste a blend of pizza and soda, reminders of the problems they faced.

She shouldn't let him kiss her like this. After all, he'd promised he hadn't come here to complicate things. But her senses pushed past her logic and she kept allowing him to kiss her. Right there, under the porch light of her home.

Stolen moments. Stolen kisses. These were her memories as a teen. But tonight, Sally stood as a grown woman before Taign. Fully aware he was all wrong for her. Aware of how his single kiss could open a Pandora's box full of woes. She had too much at stake to fall for this man. A man intent on leaving shortly after harvest, the same way he had so long ago.

The long-repressed hurt about his past action resurfaced unexpectedly. Without closure, it had remained a tiny open wound. It would probably stay an open wound until she heard Taign speak about what really happened that night. About why he'd left. About the rumor with the Cranberry Queen too.

Sally had to break away from him before she got too lost in the kiss. She gripped Taign's shoulders and pried herself away from him.

Then, she took a deep breath and said, "We're not kids anymore. I'm a grown woman. And I just got out of a broken marriage. It's too soon." She was lying to him about the "too-soon" part. The marriage had been over for endless months before she signed the official documentation. But the excuse was a last-ditch effort to keep him at bay, a meager one at best. She had to push him away right now, no matter how much it hurt her to do it.

"It doesn't sound soon at all."

"But still," she didn't bother to finish her sentence. He'd already called her out on her lame excuse. Did he have to be so perceptive? She reached up to her cheek, to the heat that emanated there. She silently thanked heaven for the dimness of the porch light, which would prevent Taign from seeing her blush.

"He hurt you bad, didn't he? Your husband, I mean."

She looked away. "Not only did he gamble away my savings, he was so sneaky about it. I didn't have a clue until it was too late."

"I'm sorry."

She didn't need sympathy. Once her heart slowed to a casual pounding, she continued. "Let's just survive the next few weeks, okay? No complications, remember?"

"Does that mean I get to help?" Taign asked.

"Like I said before, do I have a choice?" she asked right back.

"Nope."

Sally moaned as she climbed the patio stairs. "Good night."

"And like *I* said before . . . see you in the morning," he called.

Sally cringed in response. Morning, noon, and night. That's how much she'd be stuck with him for the next few weeks. She'd barely survived the evening. How could she possibly make it through an entire harvest?

"He kissed you? On the lips? And you let him?" Faith's voice rose an octave as she pushed open the door to her antiques-and-collectibles shop. Her attention wavered momentarily as she called out to an employee at the other end of the store that she was back from lunch.

She hustled behind the glass counter full of estate jewelry and threw away two empty brown paper lunch bags. A moment later, she sauntered behind the register, bent over, and ducked out of sight. "Okay," she began from somewhere behind the counter, "now where were we? Talk to me!"

Sally picked up their conversation, even though Faith had disappeared from view. "Yes, he kissed me. And no, I didn't let him." She stopped. "Okay, so I did let him kiss me. But I didn't have a choice." It was becoming increasingly clear to Sally that she didn't have many choices when it came to this guy.

"I'm so glad you finally decided to tell me. I spend an entire lunch hour with you complaining how cramped my shop is and you wait until now to mention the kiss?"

"I didn't know how to tell you." Sally leaned over the counter to see what Faith was up to.

"You know I would have found out one way or another," Faith called out, still lurking behind the register and rummaging through a box. "I've got the best location in Pequot's historic district. Perfect for gossip-central, in addition to the great shopping. Nothing gets past me. 'Course, that's the real reason why I can never ever move from this prime location. But enough about me and my shop. Let's talk about the linens for a minute . . . ah, here we go."

Faith pulled out a small tissue-wrapped package from the box and finally stood upright behind the counter. She unfolded the embossed tissue and pulled out delicate white table linens. The lightly embroidered fabric made Sally sigh.

"They're as beautiful as the first day I saw them." Sally fingered the hemstitched edge of one napkin. The softness soothed her painfully sensitive fingertips. Her thoughts settled momentarily on her old job at Amberlea's Auction House. "Do you know what it's like to handle million-dollar estates and not be able to afford the kinds of things you assess and acquire for your employer?"

"Yeah, I can relate. Why do you think I accept so much merchandise on consignment?" Faith laughed. "I couldn't afford to buy most of the stuff in my own shop." She looked around at the store, jam-packed with ornate Queen Anne furniture, precious Wedgwood, and antique glassware. "But I do know how to borrow for special occasions." A devilish glint flared in her eyes. "Don't tell the boss."

"Faith, you *are* the boss." Again, Sally admired the linen. "My mom would have loved these. They'll be beautiful for the holidays." Her sense of loss came back as she thought about the holidays. For the first time, she'd be without either of her parents. Too bad her mom couldn't have any more children. At least then, Sally could have had siblings to share the holiday seasons. To hide her remorse, she raised her chin. "I promise, I'll pay you when—"

"Don't worry about it."

"No, really."

Faith waved her off. "It's been paid for."

Sally looked at her friend in shock. "Beg your pardon?"

"Someone came in here first thing this morning and paid for them. Said it was a peace offering."

"Who?" Then it occurred to her. "Taign? Tell me he didn't."

"He did. He told me all about the kiss and how it upset you. He was looking to make it up to you."

"He told you? What's he trying to do? Get you on his side?"

"Maybe." Faith did a lousy job holding back her smirk.

"If you knew about the kiss, then why did you let me rehash the whole scenario to you?"

"I wanted to hear your side."

"And?" Sally asked expectantly. "Are you gonna' tell me *his* side?"

"He said it was an accident. It just 'happened.' He took full responsibility. And he bought the linens for you as an apology."

"He *should* take full responsibility. It was all his fault." Sally frowned. She couldn't help but fret over whether or not he'd *liked* the kiss. And if he'd mentioned liking it to Faith. She decided not to ask. With a twinge of disappointment, she stood against the counter, brooding.

"So you had nothing at all to do with this kiss?" Faith asked sweetly. Sally didn't like her condescending tone.

"No. Absolutely, positively nothing to do with it."

"Of course you didn't. You were a victim of circumstance."

"Ah-ha! You're right. I'm the victim here." She pointed to herself, right at her heart.

"Hence, the peace offering," Faith answered, in that same condescending tone.

"Still, he had no right coming in here."

"No right at all," Faith agreed, with a too-huge smile on her face.

"I should tell him so. As soon as he comes back from the university experiment station."

"What's he doing there?"

"Don't know. I only know he stole my list of things I need to do before we flood the bogs." Sally recalled Taign's serious expression earlier. "He told me I've got too many priorities with the bog to handle them all at once, and then he left. Said he wanted to check on a few things. I hate to admit it, but I'm kind of struggling."

"Struggling? You mean with Taign's coming home?"

Sally rolled her eyes, fully aware how Faith would love to go down that road. Sally turned back to the topic of the harvest.

"I mean, struggling with the bogs. A lot's come back to me about managing the bogs, but I'm still pretty rusty in some areas of the berry business. Then again, things have never been in such bad shape. Something's not right with all these problems. If only I could put my finger on it."

The cowbell on the front door rang and two older women entered the shop. Judging by their straw hats and the fanny packs around their waists, Sally could tell they were definitely out-of-towners.

"I better let you get back to business. Thanks for lunch." She stepped away from the counter, but hesitated to take the peace offering with her.

Faith rewrapped the linens and tossed the package to her. "Would you accept his apology already?"

"All right. But I don't have to like it." Sally clutched the linens to her chest and smiled inwardly.

"Now go on and get out of here. And don't forget to tell Taign what a rotten thing he did, buying you these linens as a peace offering. What nerve."

"Oh, I will."

"You do that," Faith said, then smirked again.

Sally pulled up to the main house just as Casso came out, a notebook tucked under his arm and a pen wedged behind his ear. He lumbered down the stairs toward her as she got out of the old family pickup.

"I fixed that leaky pipe under the kitchen sink."

"Thanks, but you didn't have to."

"Got to earn my keep around here sometime. Oh,

and Taign's back. He went to the barn to work on the equipment."

"What makes you think I'm looking for Taign?"

Casso laughed. "By the look on your face, I'd say you've got something very important to discuss with him."

Sally gripped the packaged linens. "In fact, I do have something to discuss with him."

"Before you do, I have something to tell you too. John Merchant caught the kids with the dirt bikes on his property. It was the sheriff's boys." Casso let out a slow whistle. "Apparently, those boys got a punishment from their father worse than jail time. You won't see them riding around here anymore."

"I hope he wasn't too rough on them. They've just got to understand the importance of the bogs, and respect people's property."

"They'll understand, all right. Not only did they have their bikes taken away until after harvest, they'll be serving time by working on every bog in the area. Ours included."

Before she could protest, Casso held up a hand. "Don't worry. They'll be closely supervised. Their father will be right by their side."

Sally didn't put up a fight. It's simply how they did things around here, she reminded herself. And this was a special circumstance. How could she go against the authority of the town sheriff?

She pointed to Casso's notebook. "Muse working overtime?"

"Yep. You never know when your next creative spark's gonna strike. This time, I happened to be fixing the sink. Time to go hide and write something thought-provoking. By the way, how's it going with you-know-who?"

"Taign? Well, he says he's here to help. But he won't stick around for long. I'm sure of it."

"But that's not how it's supposed to be," Casso snapped.

"Supposed to be?"

"What I mean is, I'd hoped you and Taign would take over permanently. If he doesn't stay, he could sell. You've got to work on him."

"I'll do everything I can to make sure that doesn't happen." She'd do her best to be sure he'd keep Misty Meadows intact. As for staying on permanently, well, that was another matter.

Casso seemed to relax and lumbered off toward the woods.

"Hey!" she called out to him. "Don't forget! In the future, when the temperature drops, you can always stay in the main house!"

He waved her off. "If a bog house was good enough for Thoreau, then it's good enough for me. Now go work on Taign! I'd hate for him to turn around, have a change of heart again, and sell on you."

She waved back heartily, but dwelled on one fact; when it came to Taign's intentions, Casso had voiced her very fear.

Sally dropped her purse off in the kitchen. With the package of linens still in hand, she left the house and headed over to the gray, weatherworn barn. She slipped through the open rickety door and looked around for Taign.

There, on a bog buggy, he sat, cloaked in the hazy sunlight that streamed in from the open barn door.

With an expression of intense concentration, he worked on the John Deere all-terrain vehicle. He looked up once and grinned at Sally. His confident smile melted away her intention to scold him. Instead, she indulged in the sweet sight of everything that was *Taign*.

With dirt and oil streaked across his face, he looked like a man who could never truly be separated from his calling: nurturing the earth. Had so many years really gone by? Or had time stood still, in anticipation of his return, after all?

Sally feared that while she'd gone through the motions of life, her heart had stood still. Had she merely been passing time, doing things good little girls do, until the lure of the bogs and all its treasures brought them together again? It certainly seemed that way now. She watched him in awe. He wore a fitted white T-shirt underneath his faded overalls. The short sleeves clung to his rounded shoulders and flexing biceps. The man certainly hadn't gone soft while living in the city. He seemed to have only gotten stronger.

She delighted in the way the warm Indian summer air settled on his skin, leaving a moist, satiny sheen. Sunlight reflected off his mass of muscles, which made them look as hard and sharp as the steel equipment around him. She couldn't imagine this man comfortable in a suit and throat-choking tie. Not when he seemed so at home in his denim attire.

Taign grabbed a blue bandanna from his back pocket, dragged it through his raven-black hair, and wiped away the dampness on his forehead.

"I don't ever remember an Indian summer like this. All the warm days and cool nights," he said. He stuffed the bandanna back in his pocket and picked up a wrench from the toolbox perched beside him.

"You work too hard," she said, guilt-ridden that she'd taken a lunch break while he apparently hadn't stopped since dawn. "You better pace yourself. The real work hasn't even started."

"Feels good. Better than sitting at a desk with a phone stuck to my ear. I've missed this."

Taign stopped his tinkering and looked at her kind of funny. With his lips set straight and a deep V in his forehead, he leaned back in the buggy chair.

"Got something on your mind?" he asked.

"Yes, I do." Now if only she could remember what it was. She recalled the gift. She held up the package of linens he'd bought for her. "What's this all about?"

His gaze fell on the linens. "Didn't Faith tell you?"

"You shouldn't have done that. I'm okay living on a tight budget. If I can't afford something, you can't sneak off and buy it for me as a gift."

"It wasn't a gift."

"Okay, then. A peace offering for the 'accidental' kiss. So, it *was* an accident?" she asked hesitantly.

"That's right. An accident," he replied, his lips pulled into a slight grin.

"Your lips happened to collide into mine." And his hands happened to find their way to her waist. And her lips happened to kiss him right back.

"Exactly." He gave her a knowing look that melted her insides. Still, she couldn't accept gifts from him this way again.

"A verbal apology would have been fine. So, please, no more gifts?"

"I'll try, but you deserve beautiful things. You've got great taste." He pointed to the tissue-wrapped package. "I don't know much about frilly stuff, but I can see why you liked those."

"There are a lot of things I like that I'll never have." Sally's gaze settled onto his. "I'm okay with that," she added, fully aware of her half-truth.

"Sally, you deserve to have everything you want in the world."

Everything? She pondered his remark. If that were the case, then why didn't she have the kind of life she yearned for? Or a decent, honest relationship? Or a family of her own? She looked down at the wrapped gift in her hands, suddenly grateful it had come from him. Was it so wrong?

Taign hopped down to inspect the bog buggy's wheels. Her relentless gaze on his every action didn't seem to bother him. He felt her eyes on him with his every move, right down to his work boots, which made his towering six-foot height seem even taller. Definitely, a salt-of-the-earth kind of guy.

Taign paused, his sculpted back still facing her as he inspected the equipment.

"That's funny," he said under his breath.

"What?"

He leaned against the idle buggy and turned to face her, his expression perplexed. "The wiring in this thing looks pretty new, but it has worn spots in very specific areas."

"What do you mean?"

"It's like the worn wiring has been helped along."

"You mean, as in, tampered with?"

"I'm not jumping to any conclusions. I think I can patch them okay, but I'm glad I caught them now before we started to wet-harvest. If this weren't caught so soon, it could have held up the berry work. We could have had an awful serious problem on our hands."

"I don't like the sound of it, Taign. Too many things are going wrong at once. All the equipment and all the sprinkler heads, not to mention the fiasco with the dirt bikes in the bogs. We've had nothing but trouble."

"Seems not much has changed since the old days." Taign shot her a devilish grin that immediately reminded her of the bad-boy reputation he'd once endured.

"But you never destroyed other people's property. . . ."

It wasn't so much her words, but rather how she spoke them. Weakly. With a hint of doubt. Her tone loaded with the question, *Well did you?*

Immediately, she wanted to take back the statement. She'd just been so distracted by this latest setback, her words came out before she got the chance to curb her tongue. She was about to recant her offhand remark, but his demeanor had already turned solemn. He'd read between the lines loud and clear.

"Apparently, your parents were the only ones who believed in me."

"I never wanted to believe that you could have set those brushfires."

Such words always seemed to tumble out of her mouth when she was around him. Again, her unconvincing tone betrayed her need to hear the truth from him. She needed to talk about the past. Get it out in the open. Perhaps her curiosity about the unanswered questions of the night he'd left town had finally gotten to her. She could no longer cheat nature; she had to let her curiosity about the past run its course in order for it to be resolved.

"What do you mean, you never *wanted* to believe it?" Taign grumbled. He turned and buried his head under the hood of the buggy. "I thought you knew me better than that."

Loathing herself for questioning his integrity, Sally tried to offer an explanation. "I thought I knew you too. But so much happened that night. I saw a different side of you. You pushed me away. You wouldn't talk to me. You wouldn't even look at me. You kept your-self hidden in the shadows. I didn't know what to think."

"So what *did* you think?" Taign's head remained buried under the hood as he spoke.

"I can only tell you what I knew at the time. My family was losing a lot of vines in the fire, but our losses weren't as bad as the other growers around here. I also knew you wanted nothing to do with me that night. And you seemed so agitated and distraught, you acted as though you were some caged wild animal. Like you were ready to burst. Looking to escape. I thought I'd done something to hurt you. The next thing I knew, you had left."

"So it was easier to blame the guy who skipped town then try to get to the bottom of things, huh?"

His sharp comment made her realize how much it hurt Taign to know her faith in him had faltered. But she was only seventeen at the time. She hadn't known where to begin to look for the truth. No one had.

Taign pulled himself up. He looked forlornly at the equipment, then at her. "I guess it was easier for all of us."

"I'm sorry. I didn't really believe it, not deep down. Honest. No matter what people were saying."

"I still figured you'd be the last person I'd have to

defend myself to. The belief that you trusted me has kept me going all these years."

"It hurt when you left."

"I can understand that. No wonder you hated me."

"I never hated you."

"And I never wanted to hurt you."

Sally passed through the kitchen and entered the dining room. She mentally kicked herself for abandoning Taign in the barn after their talk, but if she hadn't removed herself from there, she'd surely have burst. How could she have known she'd let him down when she doubted his actions that night so long ago? His hurt expression after he learned she'd questioned him tore at her.

She'd left him, using the excuse that he'd dehydrate if he didn't get some liquid refreshment in him soon. That pretense led her in search of lemonade in her kitchen fridge before he came back to the main house. What she'd really needed was a reprieve. Somehow the conversation had veered into dangerous territory; territory she couldn't handle yet.

She was about to get the lemonade when she realized she was still gripping the small gift in her hand. Taking a moment for herself, she entered the formal dining room, sat at the grand mahogany table, and opened the tissue-wrapped linens. Hopefully, it would calm her nerves. She ran a fingertip along their cottony-soft surface and indulged in a sweet pleasure that had nothing to do with berries, bogs, or vines. Envious of the skill of the craftswoman who created the intricate needlework, she gazed at the soft pink flowers embroidered on the corners. Clearly, love had been sewn into every stitch. She still couldn't believe Taign had bought them as a peace offering.

Taign! He wouldn't be far behind. She needed to hurry. And he'd need that pitcher of cool lemonade. She rose and gently tucked the linens into a drawer of her mother's antique china cabinet. Her gaze briefly swept the upper shelves chock-full of aged etched glass and simple but elegant white and gold-trimmed china. For a moment, her thoughts flitted back to happier times with her family.

As she left the dining room, something caught her eye through the entry toward the living room. There, beyond the country-style couch draped in a colorful quilt made by her mother, sat an entire computer system on her father's grand oak secretarial. The makeshift home-office had "Taign McClory's" written all over it. She ventured closer to size up the equipment. A computer station? Plunked down on her father's special desk? Taign had taken things too far. He shouldn't be setting up command-central in her living room—at least not without consulting her first.

She'd been home barely a week, and the man had already turned her world upside down. Step by step, Taign had managed to steal his way back into her life, no matter how much she resisted. No matter how much she almost liked it. She certainly couldn't deny how he'd stirred up a thick batch of old feelings blended with new. But she had to put a stop to his shenanigans before raw emotion took over and she allowed herself to hope he'd ever care enough to stay in Pequot.

The door in the kitchen squeaked open and then banged shut. A pair of work boots thudded against the old linoleum floor. She knew who was venturing into her home. The very sound of his presence made her insides quake. The very idea of him under her roof sent her reeling. She had to put her stirred-up emotions aside and face him head on.

Moved by a burst of determination, Sally cried out, "Taign McClory! I have something to discuss with you!"

Chapter Six

Like music to my ears, Taign thought, although he didn't look forward to Sally's chastisement. When it came to pushing the woman's buttons, he still had the magic touch.

"I suppose I shouldn't expect any lemonade, huh?" he called out. After all, that's why he'd come in. That, and to spend more time with Sal.

Her silence confirmed his suspicion. Obviously, she'd found his computer setup. He had had a feeling she wouldn't like it, but it was for her own good, and the good of the bogs. She'd thank him later, he was sure. Right now, however, he'd have to face her resistance. Resignedly, he asked Heaven for help with this one. He moved with caution through the doorway and into the living room.

Sally stood in the middle of the room, her face as blood-red as any "early-black" cranberry he'd ever harvested. Her colored cheeks went amazingly well with that baby blue, fuzzy sweater of hers. To tell her she was beautiful when she got flustered would only

73

make matters worse. Instead, he drew his eyes up to her face. He had to pay attention to *her*, not merely her firm curves and heavenly beauty.

"You want to explain this?" she asked, her eyes rounded to the size of big ol' buttons.

"What . . . this? It's a computer," he answered.

Sally's lip quivered and she rubbed her temple with one hand, obviously trying to contain herself. She didn't succeed. He grinned.

"It's got to go," she blurted out in a huff.

"But it'll help. Getting online is the best way to get updates on forecasts, pest control, frost. A lot of growers are connected."

"I'm sure they are. But it—it can't stay here."

"Any suggestions where to put it?"

"I don't know, but not here. Anywhere but here."

"What's the problem?" He stepped further inside the room and sauntered over to the equipment. "We need the technology. Don't worry, I'll take care of everything. If we need to log on to keep on top of things, I'll do it. I'll do all the monitoring. I'll be right here. Day in and day out. With you."

"That's exactly what I'm afraid of—" Sally sputtered out the words. She bit her bottom lip, as though to bite back more confessions.

So that's the problem? Don't grin. Don't grin. Don't grin.

"Oh, wipe that grin off your face," she said and pouted. "Where's that lemonade when we need it?"

She strode past him. When she did, she left behind a comet's tail of undeniable tension . . . and attraction. She may have avoided his stare, but he could tell his presence left her shaken.

"I'm gonna check some things online," he called out

to her and sat in the swivel chair in front of the keyboard. Anything to get his mind off her fuzzy sweater and the worn feminine denim. Even for a moment.

By the time Sally returned with two tall glasses of lemonade, Taign had logged onto the website about long-term weather forecasts for cranberry growers. The graphic of the jet stream slowly dipped and pushed its way along the map of New England, bringing with it a threat of frost. He inspected the details on the computer monitor.

"Looks like the warm weather will break sooner than we thought. We're heading for a cold snap," he said as he scratched the stubble along his jaw. He mentally readied himself for the inevitably long cool nights, patrolling the property and inspecting for broken sprinkler heads.

Sally stood beside him, then set down the lemonade. She leaned over Taign to get a better look at the monitor. Taign inhaled deeply as a reflex. Boy, she smelled good. Fresh, like sweet dewy apples plucked straight from the orchard. Apparently unaware of how she wreaked havoc on his senses, Sally read aloud the forecast that ran across the bottom of the screen.

"It'll be my first real cold hit of the season. I sure hope I'm ready," she murmured, oblivious to Taign's scrutiny of her.

He groaned. Did she have to smell so good? And look so nice? And lean in so close?

"Welcome to New England," he answered as casually as he could muster. "Nothing's easy here, especially on the Cape." With a sudden need to cool down, he reached for his lemonade and drew it to his temple. The icy cold glass felt good against his searing hot skin. When had it gotten so hot in here?

When Sally stood erect, Taign let out a gasp. Had he been holding his breath too? But why? And why did he let her get to him like he did?

"So?" he asked, unable to calm himself. "Does the computer equipment stay?"

Sally squinted at Taign, then at the computer. "I haven't had much of a choice about things lately. . . ."

"So, it stays here then."

"I suppose."

A sudden slam of the kitchen door spared him any more awkward intimacy.

"It's Casso," Sally said. She stood there, as if wondering whether to stay or leave. But Taign didn't want to see her go. He didn't want her to leave his side. Not yet anyway.

"We're in here!" he called out.

Sally stayed put.

Casso entered the living room. With a serious furrow in his forehead, he inspected the computer. "Pretty impressive. But I myself prefer my version of a laptop." He held up his pad of paper and his pen. "I can take it anywhere I go. Doesn't need a plug either. Wish I could say the same thing for your computer."

"It's to help with forecasts," Sally explained. "I admit it, it's pretty cool."

Casso frowned. "You never needed some elaborate setup before. Hate to see you kids rely too much on gadgets and gizmos. It'll only take you so far. A time comes when you've got to *feel* a frost coming on." He raised a meaty hand and mopped off his forehead. "Not that we need to worry about frost today. Not with this Indian summer we're having."

"Tell me about it," Taign said. "Too much heat can be as bad as frost. We'll have to gear up for a frost watch, though, any day now. Weather in New England changes faster than the speed of light."

Casso perked up. "You think we're facing a frost watch that soon?"

"Maybe."

"So, looks like you'll be here for a while, huh?" Casso asked.

Taign pointed to the computer graphic. "It certainly does. We'll need to keep an eye on the sprinklers, day and night. Make sure they stay intact, the working ones at least."

"Ahh, cool weather's ah-coming. We need a change of season around here. I'll be ready for some new inspiration to write. Which brings me to why I'm here." Casso turned toward Sally. "Would you kindly look over my essay tomorrow? I should be done by then. You know, look for any bad writing and such."

"Sure. Maybe even after dinner tonight, I could look at what you've got so far." Sally's eyes turned wide as bog buggy wheels. "Dinner! That reminds me! I'm supposed to run downtown and stop at the produce stand, then pick up a package at the post office." She glanced at her watch. "If I hurry, I'll make it. We'll eat around six."

Taign rose. "You don't have to cook for me. I can head on down to—"

Sally spun toward him. "You'll do no such thing. You haven't stopped all day."

"Neither have you."

"But I took a lunch break. Don't worry about it. You both have earned your keep. Enough said." Sally twirled around, her long sandy-colored locks spinning with her. An instant later, she was gone.

"Full bundle of energy." Casso ventured over to the

computer. He inspected the wires and the mouse, all the while letting out a string of grunts and grumbles.

"Sally outpaces me any day," Taign said.

"But I'm sure glad she has you back home." Casso absently looked at the image of the cold front glowing on the computer monitor.

Home? Taign reflected on Casso's words. The term, *home,* sounded alien, even as he considered it.

"I don't think she's happy to see me. Not a bit. I can't blame her."

"It'll take time. But she needs you here. To keep things straight. She can't do it alone. And she refuses help." Casso met Taign's gaze with an incredulous expression. "Around here, we pull together. It's how it's done. She knows the drill, yet she fights it."

"I understand why she feels she's got to do everything herself, but if she sticks to her conviction, it'll send her to an early grave."

"She refuses to believe she can rely on folks." Casso shook his head.

"That why I'm glad she's got you here, Casso. She can turn to you anytime. You've been a good friend to the family all these years."

"At my age, I'm not too much help anymore. Maybe enough to earn myself a dinner once in a while. But with you here now, she's got to know she can depend on you."

Taign leaned back. "I think she's finally used to the idea of having me here for the harvest. But I'll still feel better knowing when I go back to New York, she'll have you as company."

"New York? I'm disappointed. I thought you'd stay on. You sure you want to go back there?"

Taign turned the swivel chair back toward the computer and stared blankly at the graphics. "I don't know what I want. I mean, I thought I did, but things aren't working out here as I'd hoped."

"Oh," Casso said and nodded. "I get it. You wanted to ride into Dodge and 'clean up this town.' And then Little Miss Sally-Mae would be saved and she would swoon at your feet, right?"

Taign laughed at the old man's insight. "My version's not as dramatic as yours, but, yeah, something like that."

"You know, I got a theory about the marshes and the bogs." Casso settled himself on the sofa. "I don't believe people inherit the bogs. I believe the bogs inherit us. You can't own them—not really. They're always here. Always will be, long after we're gone."

He gave his thick white head of hair a good scratching. "And the bog vines, they come back year after year. Like the vines, the people who were meant to be here come back too. Eventually."

"Year after year is one thing. I've been gone ten years."

"And your return is long overdue. Things have been neglected, and they need to be patched up. Give it all a chance." He heaved himself off the sofa and ambled out of the living room. "And I don't mean just the bogs," he called when almost out of earshot.

Taign thought about the man's words. Was he meant to come to Misty Meadows for good? He kept his eye on the cold front, lingering there by the monitor. That's what Taign was doing with his life right now. Lingering. But where did he want to get to? What did he want?

He wanted to help save Misty Meadows, he knew that. He also wanted more than anything to clear up the old rumors about himself from all those years ago. But if he did, he would have to reveal his secret about the fires—and himself. And about his old man's abusive ways.

Fearful of appearing weak, Taign had never told a soul the whole truth about his dad's mistreatment of him, no matter how much it had eaten away at his insides. If he set the record straight now, it would be the first step toward making things right between Sally and him. Maybe he could even get her to understand why he did the things he did so long ago. That's what Taign wanted. It had about killed him to learn she'd had a doubt about him all this time. But she had every right to question him. Then again, if she knew the whole truth, about his role in the brushfires, wouldn't she push him away for good?

"Take things one step at a time. And take it slow," he whispered to himself.

Why hadn't he thought of that last night? Instead of taking things slow, he'd merely grabbed Sally and kissed her. Definitely not the best way to clear things up with her. Not that it had been a bad attempt. If he hadn't known better, he'd have thought she was more than happy to kiss him back. At least, at first.

But she'd been right to stop the kiss. She was also right when she said the harvest had to come first. He reaffirmed to himself that when the time came, he'd have to dispel the lies and clear his name. Hopefully, by then, he could return to New York with all loose ends tied up . . . and let Sally get on with her life.

Without him.

Was that what he really wanted?

He hated the thought of leaving Misty Meadows . . . and Sal. Yet, it was the right thing to do. He had to go back to the city. With him at work in New York, he could resume his role as a silent partner for Misty Meadows, and let Sally run things alone.

Alone.

That's what she wanted, didn't she?

Sure, Casso would live here and roam the grounds, but Taign worried about something else. He knew what bothered him. It stemmed back to the real reason why he'd invested his savings in the marshes in the first place. It had been his wild card, his excuse to see Sally again. And since he had come back into her life, he didn't really want to get back out of it. Maybe, just maybe, he'd change both their minds about what they really wanted.

Later that night, Taign returned to the barn to tend to the equipment a while longer. The trouble of the broken bog buggy and messed-up wiring weighed heavily upon him. He checked and rechecked the fixed wires and motors, ensuring to the best of his ability that they'd face no unforeseen disasters during the harvest. Finally satisfied with the day's work, he went back to the house and headed toward the kitchen, where the aroma of hamburgers still lingered from dinner. He found Casso seated at the kitchen table scribbling furiously onto his pad of paper.

"Done for the day?" Casso asked him without taking his eyes off the pad.

"Yeah. I wanted to get in one more hour before I called it quits. Where's Sal?"

"She ran out of here a while ago. Said she had to go for a walk. Just like that." He snapped his fingers.

"How long ago did she leave?"

"Been gone about a half hour."

Taign frowned. "This time of night? It's already getting cool fast out there." He couldn't help think about how she'd seemed on edge at dinner. "Hey, did Sally seem okay to you tonight?" he asked.

"A little jittery. And kind of distracted. But I thought it was because you were around." Casso grumbled at some word choice he'd made on his paper and erased the word from his pad.

"I don't think it had to do with me. I think it was something else. Like something set her off real bad."

Taign mentally replayed the evening's events. He'd tended to the burgers on the grill. Casso had set the table. Sally had made corn on the cob, potatoes, and a fresh garden salad. Then, she'd picked up a package she'd gotten from the post office earlier and her mail from the counter and sifted through it.

Right then, her demeanor changed, maybe like she didn't feel good . . . right as they sat down to dinner. She'd tried to hold her own, but Taign had sensed something was bothering her.

He didn't like her out on the marshes alone, not if she were as disturbed as she had seemed earlier.

"Come to think of it," Casso suddenly said, "Sally did get all quiet at dinner, didn't she? Shortly after you left for the barn, she grabbed the package she'd picked up earlier and the next thing I knew, she took off like a shot. Raced out the door."

Taign's skin crawled. Something *was* wrong.

"I've got to find her."

He pulled on a sweatshirt he'd left on a coatrack by the door and grabbed the only flashlight on the nearby wall. Usually, there were two, but the other flashlight was gone. At least Sally had thought clearly enough to take it with her. Why hadn't he paid heed to his gut instinct that something was troubling her earlier? He hurried outside, cursing himself for not picking up on her cues sooner. He shined his light first one way, then another, as he walked down the slopes of the land in search of her.

In the distance, he noted a small light near one of the dikes. The light stayed still. Too still. The lack of movement set him on edge. "Sally," he murmured and broke into a run.

The autumn moon, swollen and suspended above him, helped him in his quest to find her. Its lunar brightness cast a blue light onto the marshes, which allowed him to make out her silhouette as he approached.

There, amid the moonshadows, Sally sat cross-legged on the ground. Her flashlight lay beside her, as though carelessly cast aside and left to illuminate a nearby pine tree.

"Sal? What are you doing out here?" he asked.

"Having a pit party," she answered bleakly in the blue-black darkness. A gentle sob escaped her.

When he shone his flashlight on her, she glanced into its brightness. Tearful eyes met his.

"Some party. What's going on?" he asked.

She didn't answer.

"Hey," he said to try and get her attention, "it's getting pretty cool out already. Do you have any idea how long you've been out here?"

Sally shook her head slowly. "No. I was too busy with my crying jag to notice," she answered. Her body shuddered from the cool night air.

"Oh, man, Sal, what are you doing to yourself? You'll get sick out here."

She merely shrugged and mopped her wet cheek

with the cuff of her denim jacket until she shuddered again. He tugged off his sweatshirt and draped it over her. He took advantage of his position beside her and felt her forehead. Too late. She was burning up. Not good. Before he could chide her about working so hard and sitting out in the cold, he noticed a few papers scattered by her side. Just as he suspected, something more important was obviously occupying her thoughts.

"Tell me what's going on," he gently prodded.

Sluggish, Sally gathered the papers into her arms. "What's going on?" she repeated, her words slow. "Oh, nothing, 'cept my lawyer back in Atlanta mailed me back the divorce papers I'd left at his office. Another chapter of my life down the drain. I don't know, the reality of it hit me tonight when I saw these papers again." She held up the documentation, which lilted in her loose grip. She then let the papers slip between her fingers and flutter back to the ground.

Taign's free hand balled into a fist as he mentally cursed the creep who had done this to her and thought of a laundry list of things he'd like to do to the guy. He kept his harsh thoughts to himself; Sally had enough to deal with right now, not to mention fighting off the flu or some sort of bug. But he couldn't help the thought of how a nice hard set of knuckles to her ex-husband's jaw would somehow ease her pain. He relaxed his fist. Whipping her ex-husband's hide wouldn't solve a thing.

But having Sally face the elements alone, sick and feverish just prior to harvest, wouldn't help things, either. The extreme temperature changes of hot days and then cool damp nights could wreak havoc on a person. He couldn't watch Sally torture herself this way. And turning her pain inward would only make matters worse.

"Sally, I can't let you do this to yourself. You're not feeling good. You can hardly talk, and your head felts like a furnace."

"Too late, the damage has been done. I'm already chilled to the bone." She tapped the tip of her nose. "Yep. Can't feel a thing. But I have one—" she paused, as another violent shudder tore through her, "question."

"What is it?"

"If I'm all numb on the outside, then why do I still want to cry on the inside?" Like a rag doll, she dropped her head into her hands. "I mean, I haven't loved the guy for a long time . . . if you could call it love. I still can't believe I fell for someone who used me. I should have been smarter. I feel, I don't know, overwhelmed by everything . . . oh gosh . . . I'm babbling, aren't I?"

She paused and gestured out to the marshes. "Look at all that out there. Boy, I hate to fail, Taign. But that's exactly what I've done. I've failed my parents. Failed my marriage. Dumped my job. If I fail this land too. . . ."

"You won't fail. I won't let you," Taign replied. He sat down on the cool earth beside her. "Listen, you're exhausted. You've been through a lot. Got yourself sick—"

"This is Casso's fault, he got sick first—"

"Doesn't matter. Sweating by day and freezing by night isn't the answer. 'Cause the next thing you know, you've got pneumonia and then you're no good to anyone. Misty Meadows needs you healthy."

He curled his arm around her shoulder because it

felt right to do so. In fact, if felt too right. She leaned into him and buried her face in his chest. An ache throbbed in the spot where she settled her head for the simple reason that he'd wanted to hold her like this for so long.

"I'm so tired, Taign, so very tired," she murmured.

"Jeez, it kills me to see you like this," he whispered into her hair.

"I'm sorry. I thought I could handle all this, but I can't. I've lost so much too fast. So, let me fall to pieces. Just this once, okay? Please? For a little while?" Her words slowed as she sank into him.

Taign hugged her hard and a delicate moan escaped her. The moan, soft and drawn, cloaked him like a robe. He grazed his lips over her soft locks and he was a goner. His selfish delirium at holding her again was only broken by her shudder from an unexpected sob. He clung to her. Or did she cling to him? He couldn't be sure. He only knew he got to hold her again, and would stay like this forever, if given the chance.

"Taign?" she asked with a shallow breath.

He smiled as she spoke his name without ire for the first time.

"Yeah?"

"Why'd you really leave Pequot?"

He hesitated. She must be more feverish than he realized to ask such a bold question. With so much work ahead of them, neither of them had dared open up too much about that night. Not yet, anyway. But with fever and fatigue prodding her on, she'd deliriously asked the one question he'd hoped she'd never ask. What could he say? Tell her he'd tired of his old man's abuse and beatings? That he'd tired of living in a dilapidated shack on the docks, living with his dad, a man mad at the world and blaming him for his troubles? Taking it out on him and on others in the town? That he'd also grown tired of his scapegoat status over every little upheaval in Pequot. He got it from all sides and leaving had seemed to be his only way out.

He looked to the starlit sky to try and find the right words to explain. He knew he'd have to answer her sometime—tell the entire truth—but he couldn't get into the whole story while she lay in his arms now, so upset about the papers.

"I had nothing here," he offered.

"You had me."

"Did I?"

She raised her head and looked at him through velvety hooded eyes. Fatigue was taking over fast. "You could have. I told you that the night you left. I told you I'd stick by you if you stayed and faced the people in this town."

"Shhh. You should save your energy," was all he could manage to say.

"Don't you remember?"

"Oh, I remember. Believe me. I remember."

He stroked the flaxen curls that lay about her shoulders. If he weren't careful, he'd wrap his hands around her hair and haul her lips toward his in another kiss. Feverish or not.

"But you didn't believe me. You didn't trust me. And I thought I was the only one who didn't know how to trust others," she said slowly. He could hear the desperate need for sleep creeping into her voice now. Apparently, the week's worth of physical labor was finally catching up to her, shutting her down. The flu wasn't helping matters. Always the fighter, she'd probably try to continue this conversation anyway.

"The heck I didn't believe you, or trust you," he said.

"So why didn't you stay?"

"Everyone's bogs were going up in flames, and I was skipping town. That's all you needed to know."

"But I *didn't* know. I only knew you left me without telling me why," she said through a sleepy yawn, and settled in comfortably against his chest. Finally, it looked as though she was giving in to her need to rest, no matter how much she wanted to know why he'd left without an explanation.

"The less you knew," he whispered as she slept, "the better." *Still is*.

Chapter Seven

Sally forced open her eyes. She noted the painfully bright rays of daylight around the closed window shade in her otherwise dark bedroom. Reluctantly, she looked at the clock radio on her nightstand. Midmorning had nearly come and gone.

She sat up and slowly tried to shake off her sluggishness. That's when her recent memories fell into place. More than one morning had passed. More like a full day. Since she'd gotten the flu, her body could do only one thing—sleep for countless hours. Apparently, she'd needed it.

Her gaze traveled to the separate alarm box, used for the bog's sprinkler system. Like other bog owners, her family kept the alarm in the master bedroom to wake them at any time of the night if the cool evening air ever dipped dangerously close to freezing. If the temperatures had dropped too low and the alarm went off, she would have been woken in time to turn on the sprinkler system to cover the berries in a mist of water and protect them from killer frost.

She fell back onto her pillow and pondered the unusual number of broken sprinkler heads and the damaged equipment. Not a good situation if they faced a frost anytime soon. What was missing from this picture? She tried to make sense of why the bogs had fallen into such disrepair so fast. Nothing logical came to mind. If the situation got much worse, she didn't see how they could succeed with the harvest this year. Sally hoped that nothing would ever happen to the alarm system. It could mean life or death to the berries. Her veins turned to ice at the thought.

She remembered she hadn't tested the alarm system before falling into bed that first night! Going two full nights in a row without checking the system could be the one costly mistake she couldn't afford to make. She had to get dressed, had to check the bogs for frost damage, just to be sure. Even if the weather was unusually warm during the day, temperatures plummeted at night.

She sat back up. She licked her too-dry lips and forced her sluggish memory to kick into gear. Like a slow-motion replay, recent images came back to her. Although still sleepy, her muscles overwhelmed with fatigue, she tried to piece together the last thing she remembered before succumbing to the flu.

The last she could recall, she'd been alone, surrounded in complete darkness in the dry marshes. She'd been happily wallowing in her misery until Taign showed up. Exhausted from the day's labor, she'd drifted off into slumber in his embrace. She did recall waking only momentarily to feel his arms scooping her up and carrying her back to the main house. And she'd let him. Which explained why she still wore the same clothes.

Heaven help her, but she suddenly found herself depending on Taign for support, the one thing she thought she'd never do.

With a renewed conviction never to be so irresponsible again, she trudged into the shower, then changed into old, flea-market Levi jeans and a tan jersey. After a breakfast of dry toast with fruit and a healthy dose of coffee, she eased herself out into the Indian summer sunshine to check on the bogs. She knew the fresh air would be invigorating and help clear her muddled thoughts.

She braced herself on the patio. With the balmy autumn air against her face and breath-taking beauty surrounding her, she realized she'd been fortunate so far. The small town of Pequot had been blessed with the gentlest of winds this season, which had allowed the brilliant foliage to linger on the maple and oak trees a while longer. As she walked, she admired the vibrant crimson and ochre-stained leaves winnowing in the breeze, although it ached her tired eyes to do so. Then again, every part of her ached from working the land these past few days.

Her eyes hurt even more when she saw Taign trek up the hill toward her. He had a cool, casual gait and his confident stride indicated all was right with his world. No panic in his sway. As he approached, the contagious grin he shot her set off a surge of heat in her. She smiled in spite of her embarrassment over letting him take care of her. Taign gave her a once-over. His calm demeanor indicated the berries were fine and that they hadn't encountered frost. But what about *their* encounter?

"Glad to see you up, sunshine. It's a beautiful day.

Feeling better?" He tugged thick work gloves off his hands and gripped them in his palm.

She nodded. "I guess the past few days have been rough and everything finally caught up with me. I think I caught a bug from Casso," she said, adding, "who probably picked it up from a student taking a tour here on a field trip. You know how it goes."

"I'm glad to see you up. A full day's gone by, you know."

Sally kneaded a tender spot at the back of her head. "Yeah, I remembered, sort of. I slept pretty hard. I sure needed it."

A somber cast eclipsed the light in his eyes. "You scared me the other night, out alone in the bogs. I didn't know what happened to you or where you went. Promise you won't go off alone like that again."

"Trust me, it was a first and last time. You were right, I need to stay healthy if I'm to take care of this place."

"Glad to hear it. At least I found you and got you home okay." He stuffed the gloves in his back pocket and shifted his weight from one foot to the other. When he looked at her again, a muscle in his jaw jumped. Did the memory of her cuddling against him cross his mind?

Sally swallowed past her awkwardness and cleared her throat. "About the other night, um, thanks, and . . ." She hesitated. "So, you carried me home?"

He nodded. When she cleared her throat again, he cocked a suspicious eyebrow. "Yeah, I carried you back. But I know what you're thinking. It doesn't make you look like a weakling, okay?"

"Okay," she answered, and acted like his gesture didn't trouble her in the least. She continued with her questions, hoping that she at least appeared composed on the outside. "And what about you? You got back to your bog house all right, after you brought me home?"

"I didn't go back, not right away."

His response made her heart jump into her throat. When he offered no further explanation, she forced herself to ask, "So—so where were you?"

"Beside you." His eyes narrowed to crescents. "In the chair. Casso stayed too. We wanted to make sure you were okay. Or if you needed anything."

"You didn't have to." She tried hard to sound strong, but the mirth in his eyes told her he could see through her feigned strength. Would she always fail at hiding her emotions around this guy?

"I didn't mind," he told her.

"Well, I better let you get back to work," she said, ready to end the awkward conversation.

"Right, I've got to go inside. I want to check some things online," he answered politely. At least he read her cue and spared her any real grief.

"I'm on my way to check on the pump house." She forced her lead-like legs to move down the driveway.

"By the way, Faith left you a message earlier. Did you get it?"

Taign's question stopped her mid-stride at the end of the driveway. She turned to him.

"Message?"

"I left a note on the fridge for you. Goodacre Orchards has a special moonlit hayride tonight. Sort of a preliminary kickoff for the Cranberry Festival coming up. They tell me it's become quite a tradition these past few years. Faith and Mark are going. She invited us to come along."

"*Us?*" she asked.

"Yeah, *us*."

"What'd you tell her?"

"I told her to pick us up at sunset." He indulged in a full-blown grin. "Can't get out of it now. She said she'd be out all day at an estate auction to pick out new stuff for her shop. And visiting some storage places to possibly rent."

Sally wondered why Faith had decided to play cupid so adamantly by inviting them on a hayride. Her friend knew the Cranberry Festival harbored uncomfortable memories for Sally. And now she was expected to participate in the festivities by joining in on the latest harvest tradition? If she didn't know any better, she'd say Faith was definitely up to her old-fashioned match-making antics, which meant the girl was up to no good.

"You saying I can't pull a no-show on my own best friend?"

"Wouldn't be right."

"No, it wouldn't be right."

She couldn't pull a no-show on Faith. Besides, would it be so earth-shattering to go on one teeny little harmless hayride? How bad could it be? Maybe she'd even turn old, uncomfortable memories into some new, more pleasant ones.

"Then it's settled. We're going on a hayride," she said.

"So, will this be an official date for us?"

Date? She regarded Taign's playfully mischievous expression.

"Don't hold your breath, McClory."

With that said, she whirled around lightly and trekked on to the pump house. All the while, she felt

Taign's watchful eye on her. *Let him watch,* she thought, as she tried not to look forward to her date with Taign.

A date with Taign?

She couldn't possibly consider it a date. And she'd told him so. Faith merely had this "thing" about hospitality. Cupid-like antics had nothing to do with it, she convinced herself. Like Faith always said, it's what New Englanders do. That's why her friend had invited Taign to come along—so he'd feel welcome. And so Sally wouldn't feel like a third wheel with Faith and Mark during the Cranberry Festival activities.

How *thoughtful* of her.

A short walk later, Sally approached the pump house. Regretfully, she noted the small structure's disrepair. What really bothered her, however, was to see the lock on the door broken. Confused, she entered the small structure. She searched for the light switch inside, then inspected the various water pipes that served as the lifeline to the entire sprinkler system.

Some of the rusted pipes looked to be on their last legs—an accident waiting to happen, ready to bust. Her heart grew heavy at the thought of fixing them. How would they get repaired? With what money? And when? With a long-overdue frost watch about to happen any day now, they would need to be repaired soon. The unusually balmy Indian summer was slipping away fast.

Why couldn't her father have replaced the old-fashioned, unreliable, gas-powered machinery inside with more modern equipment? Disheartened, she scrutinized the rusted pipes again. On closer inspection of the valves and joints, she realized some were in bad shape from age and use, but others, although not quite broken, were on the verge of bursting, either from neglect or from improper handling.

It just didn't make sense. Her father would never have allowed such carelessness. She mentally reviewed the countless problems she'd stumbled upon since her arrival home. She thought back to the equipment in the barn. The condition of the machinery had been worse than simply worn down and overlooked. Taign believed the damages might have been helped along. What about the fragile sprinkler system? And the pump house pipes now looked to be a potentially serious problem as well. Between the stiffness in her own joints and the confusion of her thoughts, Sally couldn't think straight. She had to get to Taign and tell him of her concern that something terribly wrong was going on. She left the small structure and returned to the main house.

"I'm telling you, Taign. Something's not right. I can't figure it out. Things aren't adding up. My father would never let things get this bad. He wouldn't tolerate shoddy workmanship and neglect. Something strange is at play here." She paced the living room floor as she mentally searched for answers.

Taign rose from the couch and laid his hands on her shoulders. "I've got to agree. But wearing a path into the rug isn't going to help things." He looked down at the braided oval rug under Sally's feet. "Frankly, we don't know how long these problems have existed. Who's to say some of them didn't happen a month ago as opposed to yesterday? We've simply got to face them one at a time."

He settled Sally on the couch and sat next to her.

When he put his arm around her and held her close, a comfort quieted her chaotic thoughts and she leaned into him for support. Distracted by his firm grip, she tried to think about what he said. Taign had a point. Who knew how long ago the equipment and pipes had been ignored? During her father's funeral, Sally had been too wrapped up in all the arrangements to be worried about a bog she hadn't expected to take care of. Only when she decided to save the place did she develop a vested interest in its condition. Losing her father made her realize how important the bogs were to her. They had been, and continued to be, the one constant in her life, her one true home. That's why she'd found it so difficult to find it in such disrepair when she came home for the funeral.

During that time, a few neighbors had promised to keep an eye on things while she sorted through what to do about the place. Even John Merchant had offered a hand, probably to watch things until he could purchase the place, she feared.

John had never spoken of any problems. And Casso had never mentioned any of these little disasters on the grounds. Casso cared as much as she did about the land. He certainly wouldn't tolerate any tampering. But when it came to John, she couldn't help but wonder if the problems had happened rather recently. And the antics of the kids on the dirt bikes didn't help matters either.

She didn't want to think about it anymore. Instead, she wanted to indulge in the feel of Taign's arms around her. She rested her head against his shoulder and wished he'd never let go. It was the same wish she'd had so many years ago. She'd never experienced the kind of feelings with any other man that she felt with Taign.

"Why is this bog so important to you?" he asked.

"It's all I have left. It's my roots."

"You know, you barely have enough land to get by, let alone make much of a profit."

"I realize that. Lord knows one frost could mean a Chapter Eleven." She leaned back to look at him and frowned. "Why are you bringing this up?"

"I think you should be prepared . . . in case things don't work out."

She stiffened. "You mean, as in, prepared to sell?"

"After what I've seen, I have to be realistic. We'll need a backup plan, just in case."

She sat quietly, but like a hidden ocean undercurrent, a cold reality pulled relentlessly at her. Taign could decide to sell out from under her at any time, despite his well-intentioned desire to help. She'd have to remember that. After all, he was obviously the realist in this partnership. *Partnership.* Her mind dwelled on the word. Based on her track record, the word didn't hold much weight.

"I know we have to face the chance of failure. But you have to understand. My grandfather sold out on his family and lost half the original acreage. John Merchant's been trying to get the other half ever since. Now that my own father chose a partner, I have to face losing this place if you go and sell on me. Partnerships don't work in my family . . . my own exhusband further drove home the lesson when he squandered everything I had."

"So, now you fear you'll lose what little you have left because of me?"

Sally sat silent for a moment. "My dad should have told me there were problems. . . ."

"I guess I can take that as a yes." Taign expelled a deep solemn sigh. Clearly, the man didn't like the idea that she still had reservations about him.

"Can you blame me? I know you mean well telling me to be prepared in case this place doesn't work out," she said, then took a sobering breath. "I know it means, deep down, your better judgment tells you selling this place may be the only way out." She glanced up at him in time to see him grimace. The hurtful truth played over his face, confirming her statement.

"Sal, we haven't come to that point yet. Besides, I've been known to go against my better judgment in business. Sometimes I come out ahead, sometimes I fall flat on my face."

"So? What are you going to do about your better judgment now?"

He pulled her more tightly to him. "I'm not going to let you down."

She snuggled into him. "If someone told me I'd be here with you on this sofa, in your arms, having this conversation, I wouldn't have believed it."

"Why is it so hard to believe?"

"I thought you'd left my life forever. Besides, what business did I have thinking I'd have a chance with someone like you?"

"What do you mean?" he asked.

"Let's face it. The town rebel . . . interested in me? The girls loved you. The more wild stories they heard about you, the more they drooled over you."

"I learn about this *now?*"

"As if you didn't know!" She nudged him. "Right up until the night you left, when you and the Cranberry Queen—" She bit back her words. She hadn't meant to let them slip, but there they were. It had been so long ago, yet the sting of it suddenly felt so fresh. She shook her head, didn't want go on.

"So you heard about me and the Cranberry Queen?"

Sally tamped down the childish hurt that welled up within her. She thought back to stolen kisses, their moments alone, only to realize she wasn't the only girl he'd ever kissed. "So it was true, wasn't it? About you and her?"

"Depends on what you heard."

"I heard enough. After all, the girl didn't put any of the rumors to bed." She suddenly sensed an awkwardness between them. "Forget it. It was a long time ago."

"Nothing happened," Taign said. "Not what you think, anyway."

"What does that mean?"

He slowly pulled away from her and stood. "I did run into her on my way out of town, but nothing happened."

"You mean, you didn't kiss her? Or ask her to run away with you and get married?"

"Heck, no," he said through a laugh. "But I wanted you to think I did. I'm not proud of it."

"Why would you want me to believe the rumor?"

"I wanted you to forget me."

"But why?"

"Because right before I left town, I realized I wouldn't be able to come back after all."

"Not even for your own dad?"

Taign stiffened visibly. He refused to look her in the eye.

"Not even for him," he finally said.

"But how does the Cranberry Queen factor into all this?"

"Because I knew you'd find out. I also knew how you felt about me."

"I was mad about you," she admitted.

His gaze finally met hers. A guilty expression unfolded across his handsome face. He turned from her, stepped over to the fireplace mantel, and stared at a family photo taken when her parents were alive.

"I wanted to be sure I had no reason to come back. You were the only thing I wanted here and I had to eliminate any chance—"

"You mean, you broke my heart intentionally?"

"Something like that."

"And you used another girl to do it?"

He laughed sadly. "It was her idea. She knew how crazy I was about you. But she understood it was for the best, so she went along with it."

Sally sat back down and let the new information sink in. The trust issue had reared its ugly head again. "All these years, I never knew . . . and when she moved away, she took her secret with her. How could you do such a thing?" The mounting anger filled her chest. After all, what she'd believed about the past all these years was turning out to be one big fat fabrication.

"I was mad at the world. Mad how everyone had me pegged as an arsonist. I had to cut all ties, the quicker, the better." This time, it was Taign's turn to pace the braided oval rug. "There's more," he admitted.

"I don't want to hear any more."

"I also did it to protect your reputation, Sally."

"My *what?*"

"Come on, how did you think it looked for 'Sweet Sally Johnson' to get involved with Taign McClory, the roughneck hoodlum?"

"I never cared what people thought."

"Yeah, but I did, when it came to you."

"So, you also broke my heart to save my reputation? How noble of you!"

She crossed her arms and tightened her hold on herself. Everything she'd believed up to this point in her life came crashing down around her. For a woman who thought she'd taken control of her life, she sobered at the realization she'd never had control over her destiny, even up until this moment. She didn't bother trying to control the rising anger she felt toward Taign right now. Taign continued pacing. She knew he did so because he couldn't face her as he spoke.

"I didn't do it just for you. I did it for your dad too. Let's face it—I'd never done a decent thing in my life. But I cared too much about you and your family. He was the only one who believed in me enough to give me a job. Treated me like family. Ruining his daughter's reputation wasn't the kind of thanks he deserved." He finally stopped and faced her with that undeniably attractive imploring look of his. "I couldn't do it, Sal. I wasn't good enough for you."

Looking at him just then was like looking at the more youthful Taign from so long ago. A young man, proud, but unsure of his place in the world. A young man full of raw emotion and pent-up angst that he never quite knew how to handle.

In any other circumstance, his sorry expression would have made her want to go to him. But she had to keep herself together, sift through her own churning thoughts. "Who were you to decide? I mean—" She found it difficult to say more. This onslaught of information had left her mind in a tailspin. "That night changed my life forever. The way I looked at things. The way I felt about people. The way I felt about you. It hurt, Taign. You hurt me bad."

"It about kills me to hear how much I hurt you."

He took a deep, shuddering breath, as if to will himself not to break down in front of her. He kept his head hung low, his broad shoulders slumped humbly for what he'd done. Like a man who'd realized his grave mistake, he looked earnestly sorry for what he'd done and willing to accept whatever punishment came his way.

"You have no idea how much I hurt. It's hard to even face you right now." She turned away from him. She feared what harsh remarks she was capable of blurting out at him at this very moment. And he'd deserve it too.

"You have every right to feel that way—" he offered quietly.

"Yes, you're right, I do. And I also have the right to take some time alone to figure things out."

"I understand. And if that's what you want, I'll give you all the space and time you need."

"I need that space now."

Reading her cue, he reluctantly turned to leave, but then paused. "For what's its worth, if you need me, I won't be far. I'm gonna go to . . ." he cleared his throat, "I'm going to see my dad's grave and. . . ." He stopped speaking altogether.

His words had come out hard and fast. Clearly, visiting the grave would be difficult on him. But Sally knew he had to do it. He had to take these steps to come to terms with his past, no matter how tough it would be on him. She stayed silent and waited for him to regroup.

"If you decide you want to talk to me," he said, "then that's where I'll be. Unless you need to give me a good slug now before I go . . . I deserve it."

"You do deserve it," she said, and whirled back around toward him. "And while that sounds good about now, no, I'm not going to slug you."

"Sal, I'm sorry." He tilted his head and looked at her with solemn, black eyes. "Will you be okay?"

"Honestly? I'm not so sure," she replied.

After all, Taign had just confessed he'd broken her heart on purpose.

After several minutes of searching the cemetery grounds, Taign finally found his father's small marked grave. He looked over the sea of headstones amid a colorful mosaic of fallen oak and maple leaves. The wind had picked up, and chilly gusts of air tossed leaves into the air. So much for Indian summer. It had come and gone in a blink of an eye.

He jammed his hands in his pockets, forced himself to look down at his father's final resting place, and shivered.

He wanted to feel the painful loss of a parent the way any grown child would. The way Sally mourned the loss of her mom and dad. But the years of his father's abuse had been riveted so tightly into his memory, they overshadowed any potential for deep grief. His memory of pain did conjure up a lifetime of regret over not having had the kind of dad he could look up to, the way he'd looked up to Sally's dad. A kind of dad he could love better. But only God knew how hard he'd tried to love the man right all those years ago. Despite his attempts, the best Taign had been able to do was survive, physically and emotionally.

Taign recalled the day he received word of his father's death. He'd been too wrapped up in his high stress job on Wall Street to let it really hit him. Besides, his heart was so hardened by then, he couldn't allow himself to feel the loss anyway. He only knew the old man could never lay his hands on him again or hurt anyone else now that he was gone. Somehow, an odd satisfaction at the thought had filled him then; it was all he had been capable of at the time. And while he hadn't attended his father's funeral, he had thought to visit the grave once or twice, but decided against it. He hadn't been ready to return to Pequot—until now.

When Sally's father was still alive, the man had called him to fill him in about how a small handful of folks in town got together to purchase the small marker for a gravestone. That's how New Englanders did things, Sally's father had told him.

"If only they knew the truth about you, Dad, and about the night of the fires," he said to the modest grave, "they would have skinned you alive."

If only the townsfolk had known his father had started the brushfires in a drunken tirade when he couldn't get work. The old man had been warned that no one would hire him if he kept up his bad habits and didn't watch his temper. If only they'd realized Taign had tried to stop his dad's rampage that night. If only he could have stopped the blaze before it got out of control.

Instead, Taign's efforts had backfired. When he'd placed himself at the scene of the brushfires, he'd opened himself to allegations that he'd been the one to start it. All because of his hardcore reputation.

"Let them think what they want. You and I know the truth, right, Dad?" he asked the silent grave. It was better this way. He had never wanted the world to know it had been his father who had caused so many people so much loss and heartache then. They would have run the man out of town, and then what would have happened to him?

But it had been more than that. If the secret had gotten out, it would have also revealed the truth about his father's abusive hand. And Taign had had a reputation to keep back then. He wouldn't accept pity from a soul. No way would he have let the world know that tough-guy Taign McClory had it so bad at home. Nor had he wanted anyone to know he'd stayed at home as long as he could to try and help. So went the rationale of one mixed-up nineteen-year-old.

But his wasn't the only reputation he had needed to consider then. Sally's had also been at stake. Word had spread like wildfire about how she had more than a crush on him. As much as he had feelings for her, he couldn't cross the line with her old man. He'd loved and respected Harry Johnson, but even more, he'd known deep down he wasn't good enough for Sally.

So, before Sally's dad could hear any potential rumors about Sally and him, Taign had made it perfectly clear that his interest lay with the Cranberry Queen.

Now Sally knew the truth. What he'd done had been for her own good. So why did he still feel so rotten?

Chapter Eight

Several hours and several errands later, Taign was halfway up the driveway when Sally stepped outside onto the patio. Although she'd changed into a light, creamy-colored cable knit sweater, he couldn't help but notice those same formfitting Levi jeans she'd been wearing earlier. She was so darn easy on the eyes.

"You're back in the nick of time for the hayride," she said in an even tone as she made her way to the stairs. She didn't come down the steps, but rather stood there, staring at him with narrow, cautious eyes. "Faith and Mark called. They'll be here any minute," she added, her tone still flat and unreadable.

At least she chose to keep the conversation courteous. Yet, half of him kinda' wished she would stomp down those stairs, march up to him, and give him the good slug he deserved. Then maybe they'd both feel a little better. But he knew she'd never do something like that. So, for now, he remained at the foot of the steps and took in the sight of her. Despite her cautious expression, she appeared alert, and a sparkle flickered in her lavender-flecked eyes. Or was that a glare? He couldn't be sure. He only knew her feistiness had indeed returned as of this afternoon; surely their intense conversation had something to do with it.

"How you doing?" he ventured cautiously. "You all right?"

She responded by clearing her throat loudly and pursing her lips. He wasn't surprised. Even he believed it was too soon to be let off the hook for what he'd done. He noticed that her tattered denim jacket and his sweatshirt were hanging in her hand.

"Here. It's getting cooler now, even during the day. So much for Indian summer. Wouldn't be surprised if we had a frost watch tonight or tomorrow." She tossed him his sweatshirt. At best, they were on speaking terms. And just like the average New Englander, she kept to a safe topic . . . the weather.

He caught the sweatshirt in midair, but kept his distance. He didn't dare climb the stairs and approach her. Not when he still couldn't read her disposition. Although he'd left the house on rotten terms, he wondered how it would affect the rest of the evening. He just wished he could think of a way to speed up getting past this rough bump between them.

"So . . . is now a good time to slug me?" he asked. "Maybe it would help things along."

She almost laughed. Well, more like a semi-half-tilt at one corner of her mouth. It was enough for him to hold onto. Maybe they weren't quite at the forgiveness stage, but he didn't get the sense she wanted to throw him out of her life for good. For that, he'd be eternally grateful.

"I did a lot of thinking while you were gone." She

paused right then to bite the bottom of her lip. Could she be biting back any harsh words meant for him? It must have been hard for her, he realized, to come to terms with the truth about their past. "A *lot* of thinking," she continued.

"And?"

"It's just that . . . I'm tired of letting my past dictate my future. Especially since what I'd believed about the past was all wrong. It's gotten me nowhere."

"It was a long time ago."

"But sometimes it doesn't feel like it. Especially with you here now."

"Can you forgive me?" Way too soon to ask such a thing, he knew, but he needed to hear her say it. Or at least hear a promise of forgiveness at some time in the future. If she couldn't, then it would be *his* future that got dictated by the past.

"I want to forgive, but it's hard to forget."

"I know. And I know it'll take some time. While I'm here, I want to make it up to you. Maybe start over. Start new. Somehow. We've got a lot ahead of us, with the bogs and all."

She shifted and leaned into the patio railing. The gesture brought his attention to those feminine curves of hers. He looked up at her and saw the light in her eyes dim for a moment. If only she'd give him a sign, an indication as to whether they had a chance at patching things up. Or whether the attempt was futile.

"So, what do you say?" he pressed.

She shifted in response again, rocking her weight onto the other foot. "Look, I'm not over what you did. Let's be clear about that. But with everything I've been through these past several months, one thing I've learned is that you have to keep going and doing what's right and what's best. No matter what curves life throws you." Her gaze swept the landscape and she got awful quiet.

Yes, he could tell her concern lay with the bogs, but he also knew she was referring to so much more. The end of a marriage. A sudden change in address and occupation. The loss of another parent. And ultimately discovering the truth about the past. His sense of timing couldn't have been much worse.

He said, "Life threw me a lot of curves the night of the brushfires, more than you could imagine. I don't think anyone was thinking straight that night." He couldn't offer much more of an explanation than that. He simply wasn't ready.

"I'm trying to believe your heart was in the right place."

"It was. Honest."

"And it also helps to know that you really didn't have feelings for the Cranberry Queen. I'm sure it sounds silly to admit." She inhaled the cooling New England air.

"No. It doesn't sound silly."

She looked to the sky. "I mean, can you imagine how I felt, at seventeen, begging you to stay and tough it out only to later hear a rumor about you and another girl?"

Taign overlooked the slight tremor in her hand when she secured a tendril of light hair behind her ear. She let out a nervous laugh. He couldn't think of anything more humiliating or hurtful for a vulnerable seventeen-year-old back then.

"No. I couldn't imagine how it must have felt. I know if I'd learned that about you, I would have gone out of my mind."

She brought her gaze to him, her eyes brightened. "Really?"

"Absolutely."

After an endearing smile, she said, "I also realized something else. I've been so wrapped up in how I was affected by that night, that I never stopped to consider what you might have been going through. My world was real small at the time. I'd like to think I've grown a little since then. So," she paused pensively, "it's time to get over the past and move on."

It was all he had to hear. He broke into a broad smile and nodded. "I'm glad to hear it."

Sally let out a pent-up breath and seemed to relax before him. Even her sweet features softened. The uneasiness between them suddenly dissipated.

"I'm glad we got this out in the open. And now, at least, we won't have this—this tension between us anymore." She brought her hand to her heart.

The uneasiness might have lightened, but the tension still remained. After all, he never knew if she wanted to kill him or kiss him. He definitely hoped it was the latter.

"Oh, I think we still have tension between us." He saw no reason to deny it. He recalled the last time he saw her poised on the stairs. He'd kissed her. If kissing her hadn't caused more tension between them, he didn't know what would.

She tilted her head, as though puzzled. "Oh? You think? There's still—um—tension?" Her voice cracked. It made him smile all over again.

"Absolutely."

Her sweet mouth opened and her jaw fell. Taign could tell she was taken aback. But before she could refute his observation, Faith's van pulled into the driveway.

"Looks like our double date is here. After you," Taign said.

"This is not a date, Taign," she said, in a lightly teasing tone, as she climbed down the stairs. "It's a— it's a . . ."

"While you try and figure out what this is, why don't you hop in the van?"

"I—I don't have to figure out anything. Like I said, you're still not off the hook. I mean, um, I'm not too happy, you know," she tried to volley back, then huffed with indignance.

"Yeah?" he asked with a laugh. "Then why are you stumbling over your words?"

She responded with a dramatic turn of her head as she climbed into the van. Taign followed her.

During the ten-minute drive, Faith boasted a laundry list of events for the upcoming festival: parade, pie-eating contest, kiddy petting zoo, sack races, carnival rides, local agricultural show, the historic district merchants' display booths, and the festival's grand finale, Pequot's Annual Clambake followed by the "Cranberry Bounce" dance. For tonight, the more subdued activities included mulled apple cider and a moonlit hayride.

Faith soon pulled into Goodacre Orchards and parked by a weather-beaten, post-and-rail fence that ran along the property. The sun had started to set, which cast long shadows across the barn alongside the endless rows of spindly apple trees already picked of their fruit. Sally hopped out and inhaled the air's sweet fragrance. She thought back to bittersweet memories of apple picking with her parents and filling countless bags with the juicy, luscious fruit. Her mouth watered as she recalled her mother's tasty homemade apple-sauce, pies, and cobblers.

Taign brushed past her, catching her hand in his. He gently tugged her along to keep up with Mark and Faith. If his hand hadn't feel so good against hers—despite her residual scratches—she probably would have pulled away right then and there. But she couldn't. She still needed to figure out what was going on between them. She really didn't mind holding hands anyway. In fact, she finally admitted to herself, she had always dreamed something like this would happen one day.

Inside the barn, she welcomed the sight of longtime familiar faces who were busily making the last batch of cider for the day. Clusters of kids nearby poked tiny hands in jars on shelves to get to treasured penny candy. She stole a peek at the country-style concession stand piled high with treats: crumb cakes, pies, and donuts. Could the Goodacre family have possibly guarded their secret recipe all these years for those apple cider donuts that sizzled in vats of hot oil in the back kitchen? She already knew the answer. Oh, yeah.

Just like old times.

Taign immediately approached the counter to buy a small bag of apple cider donuts. Armed with the do-nuts and larger paper bags to collect Macintosh apples and other seasonal vegetables from wooden bins and bushel baskets, she and Taign strolled along the creaky wooden barn floor littered with piles of bright orange pumpkins. The sights, the smells, and even the sounds of the humming cider press brought out a longing within her. She truly wanted to hold onto this way of life. She wanted Misty Meadows to succeed.

She wanted Taign to stay in Pequot.

She tried not to think of that impossibility now, and instead, tried to simply enjoy the time she had with the man.

As though he sensed her wistful reverie, Taign lightly squeezed her hand. After he left their bagged goods with Faith, he led Sally out in the direction of the orchards.

"C'mon," he prodded her.

"Where are we going?"

"To be alone."

Sally's heart picked up a beat. Inhaling the crisp scent of falling leaves, she strolled alongside Taign until she found herself alone with him, surrounded by nothing but foliage-laden apple trees.

Taign walked over to a tree and leaned against it. He held her hand, then fell silent.

"What's on your mind? Is something wrong?" she asked.

"Nothing's wrong. In fact, everything's right. And I don't know what to do about it."

"What do you mean?"

"I mean . . . *you*. I don't know what to do about you. From the moment I saw you again," he said, then paused. He studied her mouth. "I can't think of anything else. I can't get you out of my head. But there's so much work to be done on the bog and we never have more than a minute alone to talk calmly about. . . ." He paused again, as though searching for words. "To talk about us."

"Us?" She had to be sure she'd heard him right.

"Since that first night, you're all I've thought about. You're all I have on the brain." He put his arms around her and drew her into him. Thrown off balance, she had no option but to fall into his embrace.

"You know, getting over the past doesn't mean I should fall into your arms so easily now," she asserted, fully aware she should keep her heart in check.

"But you're in my arms now."

"Yeah, but my gut instinct tells me I'm playing with fire." Sally laid flattened palms against his cheeks and smiled sweetly up at him. "And that I might be jumping into something before I'm ready."

Hope flared in Taign's eyes. "At least you're willing to jump, which sounds promising enough to me. The way I see it, there's one thing left to do."

"What?" She happily waited for the answer.

He brought his lips close to her ear. If Taign made a move to kiss her again, she'd be lost. Anticipation mounted within her. How long would she be able to resist her feelings for this man?

"We'll have to reassure your gut instinct," he finally whispered in her ear. His lips lingered there, making her skin tingle. She expected Taign to kiss her at any moment.

But the moment lingered too long, and Taign slowly pulled back to regard her. As the anticipation ebbed, she let out a long breath. What was it about this man that made her breath go? When she started to ask if something was the matter, he brought a finger to her lips.

"You don't know how hard it is for me to hold back from kissing you," he said. "But if I kiss you again, right now—"

Shouts in the distance called out for Sally and Taign to return to the barn for the hayride.

"The time has come," Sally said, "for the hayride, I mean."

But she didn't pull from his grip. He'd have to be the one to break the embrace. Because if she could, she'd stay in his arms forever.

The next morning, Sally woke to the memory of Taign and her in the apple orchard and on the moonlit hayride. Last night's kickoff for the Cranberry Festival didn't trouble her the way she'd first expected it would. In fact, the evening had gone surprisingly well. No denying she even—dare she say it? *Enjoyed herself?* And when the night air turned chilly, Faith and Mark had covered all four of them in blankets to keep them warm in the back of the hay-filled, horse-drawn cart. The thought of how she'd huddled under a scratchy old woolen blanket with Taign, along with a hay-throwing fight, made a giddy, youth-like warmth charge through her.

She snuggled under her quilt more cozily. Throughout the entire evening, she'd fully expected the man to kiss her once and for all. But whenever he'd reached for her, it had been to draw a piece of hay from her hair, or to rub her arms to keep her warm. Last night had been one of the most endearing, sweet nights of her life.

She frowned.

If she didn't know any better, she would have thought that last night had all the makings of a date. Admittedly, she had wanted a kiss from him. But the kiss never came. What business did she have rekindling some useless schoolgirl crush on this man?

A crush?

How could she let herself get all caught up in his

devilish eyes, his hard mouth, and his strong, manly hold? She squeezed her eyes shut. Maybe it was a dream. Maybe, just maybe, when she opened her eyes, she'd realize she'd imagined the whole thing.

She opened her eyes. When she pushed back a lock of hair off her face, she came across something stiff sticking into her scalp. She pulled at it—another piece of straw from the hayride. She groaned. It hadn't been a dream after all.

But if she were so upset about the whole thing, then why could she feel the edges of her mouth curl into a smile?

Muffled voices from the kitchen caught her attention. She pulled herself out of bed, shrugged into a terry robe, and stole downstairs in bare feet. As she got closer, the voices grew louder and more intense. Although not quite an argument, it certainly sounded like an awfully heated discussion.

When she rounded the corner into the kitchen, she saw Taign, his back against the counter, a coffee mug in his hand. She tried to ignore how he filled out his thick, quilted plaid flannel shirt, hung untucked over well-worn jeans. She drew her attention away from him and to the others. Across the room stood a young, very attractive woman with chestnut hair wearing a navy business suit. The woman carried an oversized briefcase, her knuckles turned white by her tight grip. Beside her stood John Merchant, arms crossed, legs spread wide, as though ready for a fight.

"I won't let you waltz in here, messing with that girl's head and ruining her life, right along with everybody else," John warned Taign, unaware Sally had entered the room.

Sally gripped the doorway. "What's going on?"

The threesome stood quiet. Taign wouldn't face her. Instead, he swallowed back some coffee. Although he towered over John Merchant, he didn't stand up to the man. Nor did he refute the man's accusations. In fact, he didn't do anything at all.

When Taign offered no response, John shook his head and grumbled something inaudible to the woman. The woman then looked Sally up and down with a tilt of her head.

Sally gave a firm tug to her terry cloth belt, tightening the bathrobe around her, and indicating that she wouldn't shrink from the blatant scrutiny she was receiving in her own home.

"What's going on here?" she asked again.

John pointed a long, crooked finger at Taign. "Throw him out while you can, Sally. You're father was a fool to get wrapped up with this crook. I always knew he'd weasel his way into getting this land. He swindled your dad. Don't let him swindle you too. He's trouble. Always has been."

"Please, let's keep Taign's past out of this and stick to why you're here this morning. In this house. This kitchen."

"We're here to discuss the sale of Misty Meadows," said the young chestnut-haired sprite in the power suit. "But apparently, Taign, here, has had a change of heart about his business decision." The woman paused, then shifted on one high-heeled pump. She pivoted her body in Sally's direction. "I don't know what you two discussed over the weekend, but turning this place around was not on the agenda for our little meeting this morning."

Sally looked back at Taign. "Meeting?" But Taign was busy pouring himself another cup of coffee. "Any other surprises I should know about?" Sally asked him.

"Yes, Taign, anything else you've neglected to mention to us? Any other change in our plans?" the woman in the suit added.

"And who are you, exactly?" Sally asked, undaunted by the woman's austere gaze.

"Elaine Steele. You could say I'm Taign's—um— *business associate.* We're here with Mr. Merchant to discuss the sale of Misty Meadows."

Taign finally turned and faced the woman. "No, Elaine. *You're* here with Mr. Merchant."

"Taign, you *know* Mr. Merchant has expressed an interest—"

"Misty Meadows is not for sale. And I never agreed to any of this," he answered back.

"But you didn't disagree, either. Then again, you don't have many options. You saw the numbers yourself. Your own business interests clearly indicate something's got to go. This place is bleeding you dry, but you refuse to accept it." The thin cords in the woman's slender neck pulsed as she pointed to papers laid out on the kitchen table. "We agreed the other night . . . cut your losses and get out while you can."

"I told you. No. Not this time."

"Taign, why don't you come back home to New York with me and—"

"Don't do that, Elaine."

Home? Sally tried to decipher the volley of words between them. The woman did say *home,* didn't she? Back to New York?

Elaine must have seen Sally's complexion go white, because she turned to her. "Oh, didn't he tell you about our engagement?"

"That was months ago," Taign said. But Elaine didn't look his way. She apparently wasn't finished confronting Sally. The woman held her stare another moment for emphasis.

Once Elaine felt she had made her point, she turned back toward Taign and said, "There may be no more engagement, officially, but you and I still have . . . unfinished business between us. I care about you too much to watch you go broke by hanging onto—" she gestured vaguely about the antiquated kitchen, "all this."

"What do you want?" Sally pushed up her robe sleeves and took a step toward the woman. She tried to ignore the sinking in the pit of her stomach at the reminder of the financial woes she faced. Besides, she was too busy preparing herself to take on this woman and put her in her place.

Elaine set her narrow eyes on Sally, not about to back down. "I want you to consider your actions very seriously. You can't make a go of this place without capital. And it's financially wiping out all parties involved. How can you be so selfish?"

"Selfish? You know nothing about this—"

"I know enough. I know how you tore up your membership card to the International Appraiser's Guild. Gave up your successful career as an antiques appraiser to grow berries. I'm sure you probably mean well, but you also know how fragile land like this is. I mean, insects alone can ruin you. Am I right, Mr. Merchant?" Elaine glanced over her shoulder at John.

John lowered his guilty expression and mumbled something, but the man's lack of confirmation didn't stop the woman. Again, she locked gazes with Sally. Sally didn't falter.

"What are those pesky little critters called?" the woman asked innocently. "Oh, yes, of course—cranberry girdlers. I'd hate to think what an infestation could do to fragile land like this. And what if the water quality was compromised? This place would be shut down in a heartbeat. Not to mention the rundown, broken equipment. Who knows what little disaster could arise next? One simple phone call to the Department of Agriculture and—"

"Is that a threat?"

"I can only suggest you get out while you can. Both of you. Funds are diminished. The bogs need to be flooded and harvested now. And the poor condition of the equipment—let alone the sprinklers—will make it virtually impossible to harvest your precious little berries." Despite the woman's feigned sorrowful frown, her tone held not one inkling of apology. "Only a man like Mr. Merchant here has the means to keep this place going. But then, again, maybe you're right. Maybe I know nothing about this. . . ."

Sally pivoted toward Taign. "You taught her well."

"Cranberries was all he ever talked about during our—" She shifted on a heel toward Taign. "Engagement."

Taign sprang from the counter. He took Elaine's arm and propelled the woman out the door. "Outside. Now."

"What were you trying to pull back there?" Taign demanded once he got Elaine well out of earshot. He let the side door close with a thud behind him.

Elaine eased from his grip and tottered away from him. "I'm trying to help you, whether you believe it or not," she snapped.

"That's some help you gave back there. Sally was right. You know nothing about this."

"I thought I was right on the money, from the look on her face."

"Sure, about the bog business. But not what's really going on. You'll never understand."

"No, I won't. And believe me, I've tried. You sink every last dollar into this hole in the ground while I try to give you a chance to get out. You've helped me out before. Now I want to help you. Why won't you take it?"

"I don't want it."

"Then what do you want?" Elaine dropped her briefcase and crossed her arms. She narrowed her eyes at him, waited for an answer.

"I want to see this work out."

"To see what work out?" she asked, clearly exasperated.

Good question.

What exactly did he want to work out . . . really? Yes, he wanted things to work out with the bogs, but wasn't that merely a precursor to his real goal? To make amends with Sally? Didn't he really want to work things out with her? He also had to contend with his own personal issues in order to work out his past. Elaine's question made him really think. But with so much to sift through, he'd have to shelve any answers, for now. He looked down the hill at the berry-laden fields. The bogs had to come first for now, he realized. They needed so much work; they demanded top priority. He could be surer of nothing else.

"I want all *this* to work out." He pointed out toward the land.

"This . . . what?" She looked at the bogs laid out at

varying elevations and shook her head. He could tell by her confusion she simply couldn't *see* it. She saw nothing in the land. The beauty. The history. Its very life force. What the bogs meant to the families of Pequot and their livelihoods. Only someone like Sally could see it, understand it, feel it.

Could a woman like Elaine ever understand?

Elaine squinted her eyes the way she always did when she was calculating something in her head. She paused momentarily before she took in a deep breath.

"Oh, my gosh. I get it now." She nodded in great understanding. Then, in an uncharacteristically light-hearted manner, she smacked her head and let out a gusty laugh.

"You get it? You really do?"

"Why didn't I see it before?"

"See what?"

"It's so obvious. Of course." A broad grin spread across her face. "You're in love with her."

Taign flinched as the words hung in the air. "What? Where did you get that idea?"

"Oh, come on, Taign. I'm a woman. A woman picks up on these things." She pointed a perfectly manicured finger at him. "It took me a while to figure it out, I must admit. All this time I'd been worried that this— this *girl* was trying to sink *her* claws into *you*. When the opposite is true." She belted out another laugh, despite the lack of humor in her expression. "I never saw it, until now. How could I have missed it? You've always been in love with her. No wonder things were never 'right' between us."

"What do you mean?"

"Oh, face it. I was the one pushing to get married. I know that. It's how I'm programmed, I simply pursue what I want. I just couldn't figure out why you weren't ready for marriage. And I certainly couldn't figure out why you were so ready to cash out on New York. But there it is."

Taign had to nip this in the bud. After all, he wasn't too clear on his own thoughts. He couldn't let Elaine waltz in, wrap up his circumstances, in a pretty blue Tiffany box and bow, and present it to him so neatly.

"Elaine, you got it all wrong. It's Misty Meadows and what it represents. I love being out in the cranberry yards again. I love the equipment and the land. Being a part of—"

"Part of Sally's life," Elaine finished his sentence. "But the way you always talked about her, I expected her to be this little kid. This—this child."

"She was still a kid the last time I saw her."

"You haven't got a kid in there. You've got yourself a full-fledged, red-blooded female adult." She tilted her head. "So tell me. Am I right? Do you?"

"Do I what?"

"Love her?"

Chapter Nine

"Do you love her?" Elaine repeated impatiently when he took too long to answer. She stood erect, apparently pleased with herself that she had Taign's seemingly complex situation all figured out.

"I don't know. I mean, I do know. But I'm in no condition to . . . I guess I've always known, but. . . ."

Elaine smiled in further amusement. "Well, it's more of an admission of love than I ever got."

"I'm sorry. I never meant to—"

"Don't be sorry. Like I said, I was the one wrapped up in wanting to exchange wedding vows—more like a mega-merger—even though I knew your feelings. Wouldn't have been a good start for a marriage, I'm afraid. But, at least, I now understand why you weren't so keen on the idea. And you know what? I'm okay with it."

Elaine looked out at the bogs once again. "And I can't deny it. You seem more—I don't know—at peace. You seem to belong here." She lifted her over-sized briefcase and took a final glance at the surroundings.

"Maybe you're right, but only time will tell," Taign replied.

"It certainly looks like you've found a home. You never got that feeling from the city. I could tell." For a fleeting moment, her bottom lip quivered, just enough to give away an underlying emotion—perhaps a little defeat, maybe even some disappointment.

"Elaine, I know I said this already, but I'm sorry it didn't work out. Not that things were ever bad between us."

She shrugged and resumed her hearty disposition. "No, they weren't bad. No regrets. Besides, can you imagine us getting married? And you living in the city when you belonged out here the whole time? No wonder you always seemed to be trying to crawl out of your skin in New York. Boy, you would have made a lousy husband under those circumstances. No, it certainly wasn't right between us, as short-lived as it was."

"You'll find someone special, Elaine."

"Someday. But for now, I have a client interested in this place. It's my job to make sure he's happy."

"Yeah. And could you be a little nicer about it?"

"Nice? I didn't climb the corporate ladder by being nice," she said, then paused. "I really was trying to help in there."

The door opened and John Merchant stepped out, followed by Sally, who stood erect in the doorway.

Elaine leaned over to Taign and whispered, "She better be worth it."

"She is," he whispered back.

John marched across the deck. "Think about what I said, Sally. Your dad and I made our peace, you've got to believe me. I know you've got troubles. I'm here to offer you a way out."

Sally nodded and pushed back a lock of hair fluttering in the breeze. "I understand, Mr. Merchant. It's a reasonable offer."

Sally appeared composed, despite her rigid stance and arms suddenly crossed tightly in front of her. Taign sensed how she really felt deep down about the idea. Elaine joined the older man and together they made their way down the stairs and out to her sedan.

Sally exchanged a quick glance with Taign.

"Sally, first, let me say—" he began, then paused to come up with the right words. But Sally had already stepped back into the house. The door closed behind her.

"Oh, man, here we go."

As she dashed through the kitchen, Sally refused to look back. If she did, she'd fall for Taign and every explanation he'd offer her about John Merchant and about Elaine. She knew she'd want to believe him, just as she wanted to believe the bogs meant something to him—that *she'd* meant something to him. It seemed she'd thought wrong.

When would she learn? What made her think that Taign hadn't been romantically involved with a woman this whole time? For some silly reason, she'd believed since he'd showered attention on her, he was completely unattached. Being so busy, it hadn't occurred to her he'd have some woman waiting in the wings, asking him to come home to New York. A woman with whom he had unfinished business.

The more rational part of her never would have expected him to pine away for her all this time. He'd get on with his life and even find someone special, just as she had tried to do, but why couldn't he have been up front about Elaine from the start? She'd told Taign about her ex-husband. Shouldn't he have done the same? Why didn't he mention this woman? What did he have to hide? She'd been through this before with her ex-husband, who'd had plenty to hide, and she had no plans to go through it again.

Sally bolted up to her bedroom. She could clearly hear Taign's shouts and pleas behind her. After she closed her door, she rummaged through her dresser for clothes. The sooner she got on with her day—and her life—the better.

She had to halt her chaotic thoughts and focus on her tasks for the day. Aside from the bogs, she'd promised Faith she'd help set up and organize the shop's display booth at the fairgrounds, which showcased the local merchants of the historical downtown section. It was the least she could do. The very moment the festivities ended, Faith would be showing up on her property to help with the berries in any way she could, just like the rest of the community. That's when the real work would begin.

A long, hot shower was in order. Then a brief change of clothing, a quick breakfast, and off to start her busy morning. With so much to do, how could she get so distracted by one handsome man and allow him to cause such emotional upheaval?

When she opened her bedroom door, Taign filled up the space before her.

"Do you mind?" she asked.

Apparently perplexed, he stepped to one side and let her pass.

"Thank you," she said, trying to ignore how good

he smelled while she headed for the bathroom. All the while, a jumble of words spilled from him, words she chose not to hear. She quickly closed the bathroom door before she could change her mind and listen to him.

After a long, hot shower, she threw on her jeans and cardigan sweater. She ran a towel over her hair and then combed it out. When she opened the bathroom door, Taign stood like a sentinel before her. Again.

"Hear me out," he said quickly before she could utter a word in protest.

"I can't. I promised Faith I'd meet her at the festival fairgrounds. Let's just move on, okay?" She sidled past him and skipped down the stairs into the living room. If she ignored him, maybe that would be enough to thwart the man.

He followed close on her heels.

"We need to finish discussing this," he pressed.

Frustrated, she halted in the middle of the living room and spun back toward him. "Can't you just take no for an answer?" she asked.

"As the matter of fact . . . no. Please, Sally, you have to listen to me," Taign's deep imploring tone only made her ache more to hear what he had to say.

But that was her heart speaking, not her head. For once, she needed to let logic and reason rule the day. Unfortunately, when it came to Taign, reason was often tossed out the window. If only his soulful eyes would stop boring into hers. If only the urgency in his voice didn't make her crack in two. Why couldn't she simply yell at him to leave her alone? She wanted to draw from some personal arsenal of cruel-intentioned words, but the words refused to come.

Unsure of what else do with him, she finally cried out, "Why do you want me to listen when there's nothing to discuss? Please, let me just go help Faith and—"

"Nice try, but you're still not leaving until I explain a few things."

Taign gently held her elbow and faced her.

"First of all, it's true. Elaine and I had something for a short time. But we both knew it wasn't right between us. She's worried about me, that's all. And because of that, she really does care about what happens to this place."

"She threatened me, Taign. She threatened what little I have to call a livelihood. All her talk of insects and water problems. And calls to the Department of Agriculture."

Sally kept her tone calm, but inside she cursed herself because she resented how good his touch felt on her arm. Why didn't she have the courage to get him to remove his grip on her before she lost her heart completely to him?

"She wants to protect my interests. Deep down, she's a real pussycat. She'll back off, don't worry."

"But why didn't you tell me about her?"

"With everything else going on here, I didn't think it was important. Besides, there's not much to tell." He dropped his hold and stepped back. She missed his touch already, even if they were in the middle of another heated discussion.

"Obviously, you do have something to tell if she came all this way to see you."

"We still have to do business together. Look, Sal, we learned real fast that we work together better in business than in a personal relationship."

"But you had plenty of opportunities to tell me about her and your engagement—"

"*Broken* engagement—"

"Right. *Broken* engagement," she corrected herself, the fight easing out of her. A broken engagement meant it had been in the past. Over and done with. Really, Taign was right. With everything going on, when had he had time to tell her about his personal life?

"You had a life since leaving Pequot. I guess, with my past relationship, your obvious omission of something so important made me automatically suspicious. I shouldn't have let it, but I did. I'm sorry."

"You've been through a lot and I understand why you question everything. This sort of thing does take some time."

"So, what happened between you two?" she asked. She decided that right now would be a good time to get to know Taign's past. "Why aren't you two together?"

"Elaine and me? We had a mutual breakup—"

"Yeah, but, why? I mean, I can see what you like about her. She's bright. Worldly. Beautiful. Although kind of pushy. So, why did you break up?"

"You don't want to know."

"Try me."

He looked to the oval braided rug under his feet, as though unable to face her. "I was too restless. As if I was waiting for something. I didn't know what . . . until recently."

"What were you waiting for?"

"Not really a '*what.*' More like a '*who.*' " He took a sharp breath. His gaze claimed hers. "I was . . . waiting for you."

His admission rattled her. It couldn't possibly be true. No way. No how. She shook her head in disbelief. She never allowed the thought to cross her mind, never dreamed of such a possibility. Clearly, the man wasn't thinking straight.

"Don't say that," she said.

"You've got to believe me, Sal."

"After all this time?"

"Yeah, after all this time. Please don't throw me out of your life now."

The desperate plea in his voice hit her like a ton of bricks. She slumped down on the quilt-draped sofa as indecision gripped her. Should she believe him or ask him to leave while she still had the chance? She kept her arms to her sides and sat mute. Even though she was sinking in emotional quicksand, she willed herself to hold her ground. She closed her eyes and squeezed them tight. The very sight of him only made her feel more drawn to him.

"Sally, it's always been you."

The smoothness of his voice chiseled away at her ironclad will. Why was he doing this to her?

"Taign, I can't. I—"

"Don't shut me out now."

Something crushed against her rib cage. She tilted her head back to keep the tears of confusion at bay. The last of her defenses slowly dissolved. The room fell eerily silent. If she didn't know any better, she would have thought she could hear Taign's heart thump. Or did she hear her own?

"I did it all for you." Taign's soft words stroked her.

"Did what?" she found herself asking . . . and emotionally opening up to the possibility that he spoke the truth.

"Everything. Every career move, every financial move, was to help bring me one step closer to you. If I'd stayed here, I'd never have been able to offer you anything worthwhile. So I had to get out of Cape Cod and make it on my own. On my own terms. People here said I was muscling in on your father's territory, scheming to marry my way into Misty Meadows."

"And you cared what they thought?" She gripped the quilt on the sofa more tightly.

"No. At least, not until the night of the brushfires. And until I resolve that, I'm not good enough for anyone."

"The brushfires? What do you mean? I thought you had nothing to do with them."

When nothing but silence came from him, Sally's heart bottomed out. He refused to face her. Instead, he leaned his tall frame against the fireplace mantel. She uttered a small cry.

"Oh, Taign, please don't say any more."

She rose from the sofa and walked over to the window to gaze out at the berry-mottled bogs . . . whatever it took to keep back the pain that seeped through her. But the view of the property only made her recall the night that the earth had glowed in embers so long ago.

"I want you to hear it from me. Once and for all. Those brushfires. They *were* my fault. It's a fact I'll have to live with the rest of my life."

Chapter Ten

"Oh, Faith, it was awful. Just awful." Sally hoisted a large cardboard box marked "Linens" onto the display table of Faith's exhibitor booth. "I still can't wipe it from my mind. Taign had something to do with those fires."

"Shhh! Keep your voice down about Taign and the fires. You want the whole town to hear you?" Faith plunked down a second cardboard box next to Sally's. She looked over her shoulder at the other exhibitors in the fairgrounds aggy hall who were cheerily keeping themselves busy at their own display booths. Two men carrying giant aluminum lobster pots strolled by, headed toward the cooking area for the upcoming clambake.

"You don't want to start up a witch-hunt for the guy when you don't have details, do you?" Faith opened the flaps to the box and pulled out a large porcelain vase encased in clear bubble wrap. She began to unravel the tape. "So, he said the fires were all his fault? I'm sure he didn't light a match and set fire

134

to the place. He would have told you so. There's got to be more to the story. So, what did he do exactly?"

"I don't know. I was already late meeting you and then Elaine called him. I was so done with the whole thing, I left."

Sally opened her box and gently pulled out an antique quilt with a wedding ring motif, her thoughts still on Taign. Why did he always throw her a curve at the worst of times? When would the surprises end?

Faith heaved up a white painted, colonial-style quilt rack and carried it over to Sally.

"You can hang the wedding quilt on here, and put it to the side of the booth. I'm holding a raffle for the whole ensemble." She set the rack firmly onto the ground. "As for Taign, I'd wait to hear what he has to say for himself when the right time comes. For now, let's get your mind off the past. Come help me play with all these goodies."

Sally agreed, and fussed with the soft fabric as she draped the quilt on the rack as best she could. The action charged unexpected memories of her previous job at Amberlea's Auctions. For the time being, she allowed herself to forget her troubles and indulge in the pleasure of dabbling in another passion of hers.

"I'm glad one of us is still keeping her mitts in the decorative arts." She sighed wistfully and returned her attention to the rest of the items in her box.

"Hey, anytime you need a part-time job, you let me know. I could use the help, on- or off-season. Why, refurbishing furniture alone takes up so much time. I'm busting out at the seams and way too busy to find more good help. Even the other day, I had to stop looking at available loft space down by the mills because my one employee got so overwhelmed at the shop all alone with the customers."

"You were all the way down by the mills? Why so far?"

"The mills have lofts big enough for me. But it doesn't matter. The rent is way too rich for my blood. If only I could find space close by. Maybe from some-one with an unused loft or extra space, who really truly appreciates what I do."

Sally sure could appreciate Faith's plight. She also drew the conclusion that when it came to business, whether booming or busting, an entrepreneur would always have her share of problems. She regarded the dilemma of her best friend, who now took pleasure in buffing and shining the porcelain vase.

A thought came to her.

"Say, Faith, if anyone's as stubbornly independent as I am, it's you. You know, I have the entire loft of the barn vacant. Granted, it's a mess, but you should consider it."

"Oh, now Sally—"

"Hey, before your pride makes you refuse, I'm tell-ing you, it's not a handout, nor is it charity. I love you dearly, but I'm looking at it as a great business op-portunity. Renting out my barn's loft space would sub-sidize Misty Meadows, something I could use right now. We'd both win."

"Really, I gotta tell yah—"

"Don't say anything right now. Think about the lo-gistics. I live right near your shop. Your cottage is a stone's throw away. And if you need more help, I'd be there during the downtime when things are quiet with the bogs. Come on, at least say you'll consider it," Sally offered with mounting excitement.

"All I have to say is this. . . ." Faith paused to put the vase down on the table. She planted her little fists on her rounded hips and rolled her eyes. "Sally, it's about time you offered me that loft!"

"Huh?"

"I've been dropping hints left and right to you for days."

"Why didn't you just come out and say something?"

"What? And be rude? Hey, while I'm at it, why don't I just invite myself over for supper sometime? I might impose too, since you haven't invited me to eat and break in those new linens of yours."

"But you drop in all the time. You've shown up for dinner unannounced plenty of times."

"Not lately. I wanted to give you time to settle in since you just moved back. I knew you had plenty on your mind already, you know, with the harvest and with Taign. But, sheesh, I thought you would have come around by now."

"I'm a terrible friend."

"No, just a preoccupied one. But it's okay. And yes, I'd love to rent your loft. Just wait 'till I tell you the rest of my plan."

"Plan?"

Faith scooted around the table and hauled out her oversized purse. She pulled out leaflets from the town's chamber of commerce.

"I did some research. I've noticed a growing need for artisan workshops in the area. There's been this resurgence in interest in homespun activities. People come into my shop all the time asking about classes, like canning fruit and caning furniture. Aside from the college, which is way-far-away, people don't have access to hands-on learning so much in this area. For instance, a pottery shop just opened on the edge of town. They can't keep supplies in the place fast enough." Faith's eyes widened as if electrified.

Dizzy from her friend's whirlwind chatter, Sally finally had to cut in. "But how does all this tie in with the loft space?"

"Well, I don't want us to spread ourselves too thin but—"

"There's an 'us' in this scheme?"

"Oh, yeah. In fact, it all hinges on you. Remember growing up? How many Concord grapes did you and I pick and can with your mom?"

"Thousands."

"And blueberries?"

"Millions."

"And how 'bout your dad. What a whiz with making old furniture look like new again."

"It was how my love of antiques got started." She'd learned a barrel-load of lessons from her dad about Chippendale, Hepplewhite, and Queen Anne. And developing an eye for quality came from her combing towns along the New England coastline for antiques on weekend excursions and shopping sprees with her mom.

"In the loft, we could open an annex to my collectibles shop. Like a studio for classes. We'll call it, "Canning and Caning." We can give workshops and bring in resident artisans to host other classes. Oh, it would be so cool."

"Wow, you *have* done a lot of thinking. It sounds like a lot of work, but I love every bit of it."

Sally couldn't count the number of times her mom had come close to opening their house up to artists looking to get away and recharge their batteries. She'd believed it would have been a great means to another income. She'd recognized how the place had grown so important to Casso, and knew others like him would appreciate it. Sally remembered her mom and Casso sitting around the kitchen table bouncing around ideas on how to pull it off. Not quite a bed and breakfast. Not quite a boardinghouse. More like a retreat for writers and artists during certain times of the year.

"Speaking of artisans, I also have plenty of bedrooms either to host residents or to rent rooms the way my mom always talked about."

Faith's bittersweet smile grew wide. "She woulda' liked to have seen that. She loved surrounding herself with creative types. I remember her always threatening your dad that she'd fill up your house with kooky artsy characters some day."

"Maybe that day is here."

For Sally, their brainstorm couldn't have come at a better time. With tourists and crafters visiting the area and falling in love with the town, it would be easy to get the word out that Misty Meadows would finally open its doors as a creative getaway.

"Taign is pretty handy on the Internet, maybe he could make a website and link—" Sally stopped her words. She shouldn't be having happy thoughts about him at this moment. She'd almost forgotten his latest admission of information. "Oh, maybe I shouldn't be asking anything of Taign right now."

"Tell you what, let's stay busy with the exhibit. You hash things out with him when you're ready. For now, I need you to take a huge lobster pot over to where they're gonna cook for the clambake. They need as many pots as they can get their hands on, especially for all the steamers." Faith pulled a giant aluminum pot out from another box and hoisted it into Sally arms.

"Will do," Sally said. She did an about-face and marched her way over toward the giant propane gas ranges.

But the moment Taign stepped into her path, she had no choice but to halt. She swallowed hard. It still hurt to look at him. Not simply from the renewed pain he'd caused that night so long ago, but from the fact she still cared so deeply about him.

"Sally, I've got to clear up the past once and for all."

"How can you clear up the past? What's done is done. My father never completely recovered after all he'd lost. He'd barely gotten his debt down before he died. You and I wouldn't be in this mess if—"

"I know. I know. That's why I wanted to make it up to him. So I sank every penny I had into the cranberry yards."

"He was the only one in this town who believed in you. My family did nothing but love you." She kept her voice low, not wanting to attract too much attention. She stepped around him and resumed walking toward the cooking area. She had to keep her sights on her task. Now didn't seem the right time to hash it out with Taign, not in the middle of the fairgrounds with so many people milling about. This was supposed to be a happy occasion and she wanted it to stay that way.

Taign kept his stride right along with her. "Now you know the biggest reason why I left that night. I'd already ruined your father's land. How could I break his daughter's heart too, and stick around to witness it?"

His words spilled out, and like shards of glass, they

pierced her. Her unbridled emotion cresting, she stopped dead in her tracks again, searching his eyes. "You want to try and clear up the past? Then tell me one thing. Tell me why. Why'd you let the town burn? Make me understand." She lowered the cumbersome pot to the ground, then kept her arms by her sides. She gave him her undivided attention. Yes, the time had come to clear this up once and for all.

Taign lowered his gaze to the ground, as though to search for the right words. Could he also be searching for the right answer? She only knew it had better be the truth.

"I should have called the fire department. But I didn't. I tried to put it out myself. I figured by the time I got to the phone, it would have burned out of control. Which is exactly what it did anyway. Sally, you have no idea how hard I tried to put it out."

He took a step toward her, but she stepped back, keeping the pot between them like a barrier. His touch alone would make her weak in the knees, and she had to stay strong until she heard what he had to say. When he recognized her need for space, he hung back. With the boundaries set, she picked up the pot and slowly sauntered toward the cooking area. Stopping in the middle of the exhibitor area had been a bad idea. Some heads had already started turning their way. She didn't want to let on to anyone that they were talking about the night of the fires. Why bring out painful memories for everyone in the town?

"And?" she said in a low voice. She slowly kept walking.

"And . . . my father. He was in such a drunken rage. He didn't know what he was doing. He was so out of it. So suicidal. He had problems, Sally, real bad problems. He said if he was going down, he was taking the town with him. I tried to stop his rampage and put out the fires. But it was no use. If only I hadn't set him off."

She stopped again. She lowered the pot to the ground. By now she didn't care if anyone noted her odd, stop-and-go behavior. As the truth unfolded before her, she dragged her sorrowful expression back to his.

"What are you saying? Who set the fires?"

"It was all my fault. No one else is to blame. The fires never would have gotten so out of hand if it weren't for me."

"But they started because of your dad?"

"I didn't say that."

"You can't take back your words now. Your *father* set those fires and you've taken the blame ever since?"

"I should have stopped him. Listen to me. It was *my* fault. I should have been able to handle him. I didn't need to goad him. I'd handled him my whole life. But then, things got out of control. . . ."

"Why didn't you ever say anything?"

He hesitated, not bothering to hide the hurt that filled his face while he searched for the explanation. "It was easier at the time. You know, spare my dad the consequences of something he wouldn't remember doing. You didn't see the empty bottles. He wanted to drown his sorrows. Maybe those sound like words of a coward, but . . ." He stopped to take a breath.

"But what? Tell me. You can tell me," she urged.

"But," he continued, "when you've got a black eye and a welt across your cheek from an airborne wrench—compliments of your old man—it's kind of hard to think straight. He didn't know what he was doing. He was just grabbing and swinging whatever he could get his hands on."

Like an unsolved puzzle coming together, fragments of Sally's memories tumbled into place. "Now I know why you wouldn't look at me that night. You didn't want me to see your face. That's why you stayed in the shadows. Your dad hurt you. Why didn't you come to me and my family? And tell us what happened?"

"I couldn't tell anybody. I didn't want anyone to think that the town tough kid let his father beat him, not at nineteen." He cocked his head proudly.

"I never knew—"

"I never wanted you to know."

She wanted to throttle him for keeping such a secret from her all this time and not allowing her family to help him. But she couldn't throttle him, not now. Instead, she leaped into his arms. His fast hold made her gasp, but she didn't care. She only knew she was holding him again.

"Forgive me, Sally. Forgive my old man." He hugged her hard as if to never let her go.

"Only if you forgive me, for being so unreasonable, for so long. I'm so sorry, Taign, that you had to go through it alone. So very sorry."

Chapter Eleven

"Don't ever be sorry, Sally. You did nothing but believe in me. Besides, I had to go it alone. My dad was a ticking bomb. I wanted to keep an eye on him before something like the brushfires happened." His breath ruffled her hair as he clung to her. "I wasn't trying to be some hero. I did what I could. But I was too late. I—I—"

"Let's not talk anymore about it. I understand all I need to right now."

Taign pulled back from their embrace just enough to regard her. With his face agonizingly close, it left little more than a mingling of dulcet air between them. He pressed his lips against hers in a tender kiss. The kiss was winsome and soft, while his hands felt strong. Those hands—now callused from bog work—wrapped themselves more tightly around her and hugged her harder. Hot pulses skipped through her and her sweet, indulgent thoughts splintered. She realized she no longer stood in the arms of a young outcast with a dangerous reputation. Taign had grown up to be a man who was sure of himself, and soon would be confident of his new place in society.

When they broke the kiss, Sally said, "I wish I could feel this way every waking moment. With you holding me."

"That's my plan."

"You really are here to stay?" Admittedly, she was glad. Delighted. Thrilled.

"I tried to tell you so the first night," he said through a laugh. "I am here to stay and I plan to pester you like this every waking moment of every weekend for the rest of my life, if you let me," he said in a husky growl.

"Only on the weekends? What about the weekdays? Won't you want to pester me then?" She shot him an inquisitive glance.

"Oh, yeah. But your voice over the phone will have to do until I can get back here. I'll have to go back to New York, after the harvest. Then, I'll stay there to work all week. But come five o'clock every Friday night, I'm out of there. And I intend to arrive at Misty Meadows by ten o'clock sharp. Maybe even catch a bite of pizza at the pizzeria, if you leave me some leftovers." He playfully tugged on a tendril of hair.

"New York?" She winced, suddenly pelted with the cold realization she couldn't keep a man like Taign. She never could. How could she have let it slip her mind he would return to his "real" life back in New York? With reckless abandon she pushed back the thought. She knew he was here to stay, even if it would only be for part of the time. With everything he'd been through, she knew to believe in his decision. Together, they'd make the bogs a success.

He stroked her hair, as though to reassure her. "I

have to go back to New York so I can fund this place. We have to keep it financially afloat somehow for the harvest."

"Oh, I have good news about finances. I'm renting the barn loft to Faith. And we're going to host workshops and artisans in residence. I'll be helping out with her shop too."

"You mean in place of berry growing? That's a great idea!'

"No, silly. The income will subsidize the bogs year-round. See? Everything's working out for the best."

His suddenly looked crestfallen.

"What is it?"

"Sally, your idea is great. Business would be booming for you in no time. Between your home and barn, overhead will be minimal. . . ."

"Which will help with the bogs."

"Yeah, I'm sure those things will help, and they're good ideas, but. . . ." his words trailed off.

"But what?"

"Wouldn't you like to pursue those interests full time?"

"Wait a minute. You don't think my ideas of subsidizing the bogs will help? But my dad was on his way to turning the place around. He always got by."

"Yeah, but that was before all these problems—"

She couldn't miss how a look of regret touched his face. She didn't like what she saw in his disheartened expression.

"My family's done it before; I'll do it again," she affirmed. "This time is no different."

"You have every right to believe that, but this time *is* different. Very different."

Taign's grim expression got Sally worried. She knew he had more to reveal.

"Don't you believe in me?" she asked.

"I believe in us." He reached for her.

"Oh, no, you don't. You're trying to distract me. So, tell me. What's wrong? Give it to me straight."

Taign expelled a burdensome breath. "All right. I'll level with you. When Elaine called earlier, she gave me an update on the numbers. Things are worse than you or I imagined. And as far as I see it, the problems have set us so far back, I can only hope to do what I can to keep from losing the place altogether."

She eased out of his grip, the new information finally taking its toll. Despite her naïve optimism and solutions, despite turning a blind eye to reality, the latest cold hard facts proved once and for all that Misty Meadows could not be turned around. She got it now. But for someone with an extensive background in appraisals, she found it difficult to believe her property could be so unworthy of labor.

"Worse than we thought? How can that be?"

"The newest numbers show the future debt is beyond salvageable. We can't ignore them. I know what I'm talking about. Part of my job as an analyst in New York is to dissect a business, piece by piece, to see if it's a good investment or not."

She already knew the sentimental value of the place. Priceless. But logistically, she had to face the facts. As far as making a profit in the berry business, the time had come to be realistic. She'd seen more than her share of bogs abandoned due to the very predicament she found herself in. Maybe she hadn't been ready to face the truth before. Maybe she'd held onto a glimmer of hope a little too long. Although she knew deep down she'd always have to face the possibility of ultimately losing the bogs, the blow came as no less devastating.

"And so, Misty Meadows is officially a dog?" she asked sadly.

"At the rate this place is going, no harvest will ever pay for itself. At least not in the foreseeable future. I call it as I see it. Sally, you're a smart girl. I know your heart is attached to the place. I know you want to stay an independent grower. But realistically, if you do, you'll lose everything. That's why I'm going back to New York. Subsidizing you is the only way."

Subsidizing me? His solution took her by surprise. He was a Wall Street whiz kid. He knew better than to hang onto a dog and lose money.

"So, you plan to work in New York so you can throw money my way despite your misgivings? Just so I can live out a pipe dream? Now who's being the unrealistic one?"

"It's the only way for you to stay here."

Sally hammered down the renewed urge to cry. Wasn't it bad enough he'd had her heart and soul wrapped around his little finger? Did he have to clutch her livelihood within his fists as well? Despite her conflicting emotions, she reaffirmed an ironclad will to work as an independent grower until the end of this harvest. Being independent till the very end meant going out with some dignity for her family, to show it wasn't all in vain. It also meant having no more financial ties to Taign. She couldn't watch him subsidize her future.

"Taign, promise you won't put another dime of your hard-earned money into this place just to try and keep me here. It's hard enough that I'm falling for you all over again, but I don't want to be treated like a kept woman. It's too big an obligation."

She spoke firmly to make her point clear. She could no longer deny the truth . . . she was falling in love with him. But to have him throw money her way in a futile attempt to save a sinking ship, well, that went against every independent moral fiber of her being.

"You're falling for me? Really?"

When she noticed a spark of hope in his eyes, she looked away. But her attempt at not facing him made for a poor emotional barrier.

"All over again?" he added for emphasis

"I tell you not to turn me into a 'kept woman' and you have to go and focus on the 'falling' part?" She coyly kicked at the gravel under her feet and listened intently for his response. Why did she have to spill her guts?

"Look at me Sally."

"No."

"Why not?"

Embarrassment burned her cheeks. Taign tenderly placed his index finger under her chin and made her face him. While she couldn't recant her words, she could stop him from hoping she'd let anything come of her feelings. Feeling love for someone and acting on it—like hoping for a commitment of some kind—were two completely different things. Apples and oranges, in fact. Despite the truth in her heart, she had to keep her emotions separate from the dealings of Misty Meadows.

"Sally," Taign began, "let's not worry about what'll happen in New York. Let's get through harvest in the next couple weeks. In fact, I've got to get back to the main house this minute. The scheduled trucks will be arriving soon. I've got the cranberry elevator and water beaters almost ready. The guys from town will be showing up to help out too."

Sally's thoughts were still on the idea of Taign's subsidizing her. She already knew she couldn't have that. In fact, if she didn't nip this in the bud, her guilt over his actions would consume her. Having Taign tangled up in her affairs had already made it hard to think straight. She needed to preserve her mental and physical energy for the harvest.

"Okay, then, have it your way," she finally answered. "Let's get through the harvest. But let's get one thing straight. From here on in, we keep it all business, so we don't, well, have any more distractions. Finishing out the harvest is the least I can do. With any luck, it'll pay down the debt," she continued calmly.

"You and me . . . all business, huh? You mean for today?"

"I mean for the entire harvest." Gosh, it hurt just to say it. Her terms were a last-ditch effort to keep him from spending another penny. If her plan didn't work, then she feared she'd do something awfully stupid, like confess she was more than already falling for him. More like, she was hopelessly in love and wanted to beg him not to leave.

A thick silence filled the air around them. Apparently perplexed by her request, Taign smoothed a flattened palm down along the planes of his face and scratched at his jawline.

"What happens to us after the harvest?"

"I haven't thought that far."

"Not exactly the answer I was hoping for. So much for falling for me."

A dash of pain flared in Taign's eyes. Slowly, he took a single step toward her. His towering frame made her spine go rigid. Was he upset?

"I've done everything I could to prove I won't let you down. And you want me to stay all business, even after you tell me your true feelings?" he asked, his voice low and full of resignation.

"It's the only way I can think clearly with you around. Acting on emotions is what landed me in this very spot in the first place. It's the only way I can survive harvest. I mean, you make things . . . confusing."

Especially when I want you to stay here full time and for good.

"Sally-Marie-Johnson, you're about the most stubborn woman I ever—" He set his mouth in a thin line to physically restrain himself from scolding her any further. "Listen and listen good. I can't make any promises about acting all business with you. But if that's what you want. . . ."

"I do."

After her affirmation, she remained steadfast and defiant despite her urge to run into his arms. It was for his own good. And hers.

Taign walked past her and stalked off to his SUV.

"So he walked off? Just like that?" Faith asked while she tottered along the small aisles of her over-crowded antiques-and-collectibles shop. With a feather duster in hand, she passed the front door and turned over the "Open" sign so it said "Closed" to the outside world. She breathed a sigh of relief.

"Not 'just like that.' We hashed things out plenty before he walked. I didn't exactly give him a choice,"

Sally said as she flopped down into a wing-back chair. "I let him go. He kept springing these surprises on me. First, Elaine. Then, brushfires. And then the updated financial problems. I couldn't handle any more. I guess I realized the last thing I need right now is Taign tearing my heart to pieces on top of him having controlling interest in Misty Meadows." She chose not to go into how the future of the cranberry yards looked bleaker than ever.

"So then what happened?" Faith asked.

Sally sighed and considered the events of the rest of the afternoon while she helped Faith with her display booth. She talked about how Taign and a handful of men tended to a flooded bog while she and Casso cared for the aged pump house. She relayed these and other mundane events to her friend, including her stop at the hardware store around the corner from Faith's shop. The errand had led her to this visit with Faith and the opportunity to vent for a full five minutes before she returned to the bogs.

"When I left, Taign and the guys were about to take a break. I figured it was a good time to make myself scarce. So that about sums up my day with Taign to this very point in time," she stated casually.

Faith aimed the feather duster at Sally. "In other words, you both avoided each other like the plague."

"We both know we have too much to do right now with the harvest to be anything but all business. I was just around the corner at the hardware store and figured I'd stop by. I admit, I needed the mental break."

She slumped deeper into the chair and thought about Taign's behavior earlier. Despite the occasional run-in with him the rest of the day, he'd managed to keep his distance—both physically and emotionally. Isn't that what she'd asked of him? To be all business? And yet, the undercurrent of tension between them had been undeniable. She couldn't see him without remembering what it felt like to be in his arms. Or how good she'd felt nestled against him. Occasionally, she caught a soulful glance from him as well. Despite how they'd left things, they tried to behave themselves and concentrate on the pesky ailments of the property.

"You know, Faith, something's not right about the harvest this year."

"How so?" Faith asked as she dusted knick-knacks and glassware.

"John Merchant showed up to help today. Of all people. Even though I believe he's determined to have the land for himself. Why would he do that when he knows how I feel about him?"

Misty Meadows couldn't stand on its own two feet, but because it was adjacent to John Merchant's property, it could be saved through him. Yet she'd have to hand over the land to a man her father had never liked or trusted, despite what John professed. The man's clandestine actions and business deals over the years spoke otherwise, not to mention his periodic attempts to gain her father's land.

"You think John Merchant wants to keep his interests healthy before he swoops down on the place?"

"Maybe." Sally puckered her lips. "But I really don't know. And then there's the machinery. Sure it's old, but it's always been reliable. My father built his own equipment the way most growers do. And he always maintained it. But right now, lots of things are falling apart. No way could it all have happened in the short time my dad's been gone."

Faith froze. She turned to her friend. "You think

things are tampered with? You think John Merchant is capable of such a thing?"

"I don't know. It's just that, well, everything seems so neglected. Beyond neglected. For example, let's take the cranberry elevator, our latest problem."

"The conveyor-belt-thingy that carries the berries up into the trucks?"

Sally laughed. Her friend had lived on the Cape her whole life, but she'd always known a lot more about antiques than berries.

"Granted, the elevator's pretty old. It doesn't even have an automatic shut-off feature. The equipment should be good enough for now, but. . . ."

"But what?"

"I overheard Taign yelling up a storm about it being a temperamental, stubborn thing—"

"You sure he wasn't talking about you?" Faith shot her a wide-eyed, accusatory look.

"Yes, I'm sure. You should have heard how he carried on about the machinery not shutting off right. I've never known of such a thing happening, not where my father was concerned. He'd never let equipment go bad. No way."

"Can't be good," Faith said while she continued to dust.

"Not good at all. And not safe either. Then again, equipment does break down and farm accidents do happen." She recalled a time when Taign had had a run-in with a water-beater in the middle of a flooded bog. It was her mom who had tended to him until paramedics forced his dislocated shoulder back in place. "In fact, accidents happen all the time. But still . . ."

She paused to take a mental inventory of all the

recent setbacks they'd experienced. The bog buggy. The pump house. The excessive number of sprinkler heads. The cranberry elevator.

"I never recall my dad having had these kinds of problems all at once. To make matters worse, we'll probably have to keep an eye out for frost tonight too. I'm telling you, it's one crisis after another."

"A crisis can bring people together, which, by the way, sounds like the case here. Couldn't you say this little crisis has brought you together with anyone special? Hmm?"

"I appreciate the optimism, but it's actually had the opposite effect. Having Taign around when all these problems are happening is hard. It's like throwing salt into an open wound, you know?"

"These little incidents do sound suspicious. Maybe someone doesn't want things to go smoothly for you."

"Yeah, someone like John Merchant," Sally replied.

"Or someone like Taign McClory," Faith added.

The thought crushed her. "So much for optimism!"

"Hey, I'm just playing devil's advocate here. I mean, the troubles did start around the time he came to town. And he's already said your idea to rent your barn loft to me and offer canning and caning classes wouldn't be enough."

"Oh, Faith. You don't think Taign's got anything to do with this, do you?"

"Honestly? No. At least, no more than John Merchant."

"You're not very reassuring here. Especially when you throw John's name onto the table. They were actually talking about the sale of Misty Meadows for a while. My father would turn over in his grave if he knew."

Faith stopped dusting.

"I'm not sure if your dad would mind as much as you think. I mean, a lot's changed since you left. You haven't been around long enough to see it. I know all this has happened to you so suddenly, and it's got your head spinning, but you need to understand your dad and John were okay in the end. I saw it for myself."

"It's so hard to imagine."

"I'm sure it is. But then again, I do recall how you mentioned Taign and his little business associate lady did want to sell. Maybe Taign still wants to, and this is a way to do it and still look good in your eyes. I mean, maybe he tinkers with all this equipment, but does he actually fix anything?"

Sally couldn't believe Taign would do such a thing. "He fixes what he can. I'm sure of it. We all do. Me. Taign. Casso. We're constantly fixing something on the property."

"If you say so."

"He wouldn't go that far."

"I don't think he would either, but some people in town may think otherwise."

With the sunset near and a bog full of men bound to be hungry, Sally returned home from her short break with Faith. She'd reluctantly agreed to let Taign and the men do a few final tasks for the rest of the afternoon. And she had no problem with laying out a well-deserved meal for them.

Besides, she'd hesitantly sampled some of the men's culinary feasts at past events like the Cranberry Festival and thought it best to do some of the cooking herself. Admittedly, it helped that several wives and girlfriends had dropped off enough casseroles to feed an army for a week, in addition to her own hearty beef stew. As she'd constantly been reminded, that's how things were done here in New England.

Halfway up the patio stairs, she paused momentarily to delight in the autumn beauty of Misty Meadows. The day had blazed red with the glory of cranberries under a crisp palette of ephemeral blue and white-clouded skies. And now, a light haze settled over the bogs, as if to tuck them in for the night. Against this backdrop, men in waders trudged through the flooded bogs, wet-harvesting the fruit. Surrounded in a riot of red, they systematically paddled and corralled a batch of the bobbing cranberries with the aid of bright yellow wooden booms that floated around them.

The corralled-in berries wended their way over toward the cranberry elevator. The conveyor belt then lifted the berries high into the air before it dumped them into the large trailer truck. A cascade of free-falling berries dropped from twenty feet into the depths of the back of the immense vehicle.

The sight reminded her of the ascent of a too-large roller coaster that rose into the sky before it plummeted down the other side. Much like the emotional roller-coaster ride she experienced with Taign. She silently gave thanks that the temperamental machinery worked smoothly on this chilly afternoon and hoped it continued to do so. But she knew a long cold night probably lay ahead.

Once in the kitchen, she inspected the crock pot of slow-cooked beef stew. While a few casseroles warmed in the oven, she brought plates, bowls, and glasses from the cabinets into the dining room, the one place large enough to hold the crowd of men. But her attention soon shifted to the china cabinet.

With the last fork in place, she gave in to her desire to see her special antique linens once again. Slowly, carefully, she pulled open the drawer of the one-hundred-year-old cabinet to reveal the tissue-wrapped treasure. She sat down at one place setting, unwrapped the tissue, and gently raised an embroidered napkin to her face.

Quietly, Sally cherished the treasure. Would she build her own memories of family gatherings with the linens set at the table one day? Sally loved the thought. But she loved more than just the small, embroidered fabric squares. She loved the idea of a home with a family of her own.

The cold reality set in. A family was not in her future anytime soon. Sally set the linens back on the tissue. She gazed wistfully at them one last time and tried to ignore the lump in her throat.

When a pair of feet stomped through the kitchen door, she quickly pulled herself together. From the sound of the steel-capped heels that cracked against the floor, she knew Taign had come into the house.

Not ready to see him, she hid her treasure and planned to make her escape toward the upstairs where she could freshen up. As she passed Taign's computer, she noticed a legal-sized document jutting out from other reports from the university experiment station.

She withdrew the document. She inspected the paper twice to be sure she had read it right. A hard knot balled in the pit of her stomach.

It was a contract with a signed Letter of Intent to sell Taign's share of Misty Meadows to John Merchant.

Chapter Twelve

"Sally?" Taign called out from behind her.

Sally pivoted on one foot to see him there in a battered ski vest, sweater, and jeans. His cheeks were ruddy from the cool temperature outside, and his thick black hair glistened with a moist sheen after a hard day's labor. How could she long to hold him, yet want to confront him at the same time?

"What's with this?" She held up the documentation, determined not to shed another tear in front of this man. Where had it gotten her before?

"It's your ticket out. All you have to do is sign it. Part of my deal with your dad is to get your approval on any transaction."

She looked back down at the Letter of Intent and noted the vacant space above her name laid out in type. The place reserved for her signature.

"Selling your half right now to John Merchant is my ticket out? You're going through with this? Right in the middle of the harvest?"

"No . . . I mean . . . I wasn't going to do anything

159

until we sat down to talk about this option. Maybe have some restrictions."

"Restrictions? On who? You already signed the Letter of Intent." She pointed to his signature on the paper. "Looks to me like you've got your mind set."

"I thought I'd make arrangements as soon as possible to do what's best for you and Misty Meadows before you lose a single acre of this place. John's gonna come in here any minute. But he doesn't even know about this yet, okay?"

Sally swallowed hard. Despite his honest intentions, she couldn't stop Misty Meadows from slipping through her fingers, right along with her chances for independence at least for one final harvest.

"I can't believe you'd sell out to John, of all people." She dropped the papers to the desk and headed for the staircase. She stopped short of climbing and turned her imploring gaze on him. "I know your plan makes sense, but please . . . reconsider. Please, sell out to me."

"I can't."

"You mean, you *won't*."

"I mean, I *can't*. Besides, I made a promise to your dad—"

"Break it."

"And help you dig your own grave? Selling to you would financially drive this place into the ground even faster. Come on. Let's not do this." He caught her by the arm before she could flee. Long, strong fingers, which had gently held her earlier, now clutched around her to keep her put.

"John's got the equipment you need. And the funds and man power. He wants to see this place succeed as much as you do. This way you'll stand a chance. Before you lose your house too."

"I'm sure he does want this place to succeed. It'll add to his bottom line. And I'm sure things will turn out better for him than for my grandfather and father. And me."

She raised her chin a notch as she prepared herself for Misty Meadows to be swallowed up whole. She knew the time would come, but did it have to be this very moment? Couldn't they at least finish this one harvest? Couldn't she finish one chapter in her life on her own terms? Without ending in another failure just yet? Just once?

"I know your family has seen this land dwindling for decades, but it'll be different this time—"

"I'm sure it will." She gave him a meager smile. Surely, Taign couldn't miss the defeat in her eyes. He dropped his grip on her wrist.

"I thought you'd want this, Sally. After all your talk about us staying all business, I thought you wanted to be rid of me." He turned his back on her and scooped up the paperwork. With the document in hand, he slowly shook his head. "I desperately want to fix things, but I only make it worse. Why do I keep getting it wrong?"

"Because it can't be fixed," she offered.

He turned toward her. "You really believe we can't fix this now?"

Sally couldn't tell if he was referring to them or Misty Meadows. She decided to try to avoid the emotionally dangerous territory of their relationship and stick to the matter of the bogs.

"Sure, we can fix our problem. I sign the Letter of Intent and you go back to New York. And maybe you're right. Maybe I'd get to keep my home, but I wouldn't have you."

Quickly, she turned, but as she tried to escape Taign, his grip suddenly landed on her arm once again. Determined not to let on how his touch alone seared her, she choked back a gasp.

"You can't run away every time things get—" He stopped.

She glanced up at him. "Things get . . . what? Personal? Serious? Contentious? What?"

"Heated," he muttered. "Running off doesn't help. Trust me."

Locked by his overpowering hold, Sally stood poised. "I need time alone with my thoughts. It's how I deal with things," she said.

"Remember, you don't have to go through this alone. You have me here to help you."

"For how long?"

He didn't answer. Instead, he lowered his gaze to her arm, as though he suddenly realized how firmly he held her. He let go.

She stepped back and shot him a wary glance, as if to dare him to come after her again. When he stayed put, she turned away from him and entered the kitchen. Grabbing her jacket on the way, she walked out the door.

Sally stepped onto the patio only to immediately notice where Taign had hung his waders—evidence of his hard day's work. Simply another sign of how he'd worked his way into every layer of her life. Would everything always remind her of Taign? Even now, she couldn't stop mulling over his accusation from moments ago. She always ran away, huh? Is that what she'd been doing? Yes, she realized.

She looked out at the rest of the men still in their waders who now approached the house.

John Merchant led the way.

Fear filled her. The very thought of ever selling to the man felt like an utter betrayal to her father. She didn't care that John had supposedly made his peace with her dad. In her opinion, showing up in her home with Elaine, the business associate in the power suit who made serious threats, was not the action of a man with noble intentions.

She advanced down the driveway, all the while looking out at the shadowy pines and maples as dusk quickly descended. Now that she stood in the chill of the night air, she realized she needed a place to go. She needed direction. She had to think of a purpose for hiking with such determination.

When one of the men called out to her and asked her destination, she quickly called back, "the pump house." It was a perfect answer. Following the patch-job she and Casso had done on the water pipes earlier, a last checkup of the joints and valves before nightfall seemed logical. She'd have to make sure she could fire up the old pumps and motors if necessary. After all, the experiment station would issue a frost alert once the temperature plummeted. She could feel it. The bogs that had not been flooded yet would need protection.

"Sally! Can I talk with you a minute?" John Merchant's scratchy voice called out.

She halted. Against her better judgment, she reluctantly turned back around to see him close the gap between them. She readied herself for what the older man had to say.

He stood erect, his whiskered mouth set. "You know I'm not a man of too many words. But I think you should know something." He cleared the scratchiness from his throat. "I'd have to say, I was wrong about Taign. The boy's grown up. He even told me the truth about the night of the fires. It was hard for him. I think he was more worried about me being all ticked off at his dad."

"He told you?"

"Believe me, it wasn't easy. Can't say I was too pleased, neither. One thing hasn't changed about that boy . . . his darn pride." John adjusted his waders, obviously uncomfortable with the discussion. "Anyway, give him a chance. He's trying. Sure, he mighta' fouled up some, but I know he's got it for you good." He shifted his stance and looked up the driveway at the house. "I also happen to know he'd sell his portion to me—"

Sally's eyes widened. She knew there was more to the story. "He told me he never said anything to you about the Letter of Intent," she said. She mentally chastised herself for almost believing this man's kind words. His attempt at convincing her to go easy on Taign had an underlying hidden agenda—buying Misty Meadows. Of course.

"Before you go off half-cocked, he didn't say a thing to me. I saw it for myself. I was with Casso inside the house. He showed me Taign's computer and moved around some paperwork. I saw the papers plain as day. I didn't mean to. It was just there for the viewing."

"This whole thing keeps getting worse and worse."

"Now don't think that way. Look, I know how much this place means to you. And I do hope things'll work out. Taign is there for you. Why else would he put his career on the line and risk losing his shirt for what might amount to no more than an abandoned swamp after this harvest . . . respectfully speaking, of course."

"What do you mean, losing his shirt? I know he invested his savings and would like to cut his losses. . . ."

"According to his business associate, Elaine, he's already lost more than his savings. It's his whole investment portfolio. His job's next if he's not careful. He knows if he goes through with the harvest this year, it's gonna do him in, but he doesn't seem to care. He's also risking anything else in his name to see this one harvest through."

"You mean, he's risked *everything?*" *For this one harvest alone?*

"Sure, it's a gamble. . . ."

The word *gamble* again. She couldn't have Taign taking any more gambles. Not when he stood to lose so much, right down to his livelihood. Why should they both lose everything they'd worked so hard for?

"Elaine told you all this? Why? What's in it for her?"

"You kidding? She wants nothing more than for him to cut his losses, get him out of here, and back to New York, back to her . . . even though she knows it probably won't happen. She's not one to accept defeat lying down. But she did tell me he's given it all up. He's even got someone lined up to buy his Land Rover for quick cash to help with this year's harvest. She's awful upset. She doesn't want to see him throw it all away."

"Neither do I. Why would he do such a thing?"

John rolled his eyes at her. "For you, of course!"

"But to lose everything he's worked so hard for? That's crazy."

"People do crazy things when they're in love, and trying to make up for the past," John said as he ambled toward the house. "Thought you ought to know!" he called out over his shoulder.

Sally's feet remained firmly rooted to the ground. It was bad enough Taign had her heart and soul wrapped around his pinky finger. Plus fifty-one percent of her family's business. He'd finally convinced her he'd be there for her, for the long term, and she couldn't be happier. But he had never let on just how much he had thrown his own entire future livelihood into the mix. Did he have to sacrifice everything he'd worked for just to see this one harvest through? Including his career? Why did he insist on making it so impossible for her to resist him?

And all his talk about plans to stay in New York to help fund this place. This *swamp!* With the way things were going, Taign wouldn't even have a job to go back to. Sally wondered when he planned on sharing this with her. *Never,* she realized.

"Stubborn fool," she murmured. Trouble was, she found herself in love with him all the more for it. A fierce shiver shot through her and reminded her of her destination: the pump house. She had to get back to it to double-check the pipes to be sure everything would hold up enough for the long night ahead. She had to finish the task before she approached Taign about his hair-brained scheme of saving her at all costs. The crazy notion brought a smile to her face.

In the growing darkness, she followed the sandy path to the pump house and unlocked it. She had barely gripped the door and opened it when she heard footsteps crunching on leaves behind her. She turned and found herself face to face with Taign's immense frame still clothed in his unzipped ski vest. She looked up at him in time to see his gaze settle on her possessively.

Surprised by his sudden arrival, she tried to regain her senses while Taign placed his flashlight on the shelf just inside the door and hauled her inside with him. She couldn't help but notice how the flashlight's brightness cast sharp shadows across the chiseled features of his face. Although breathless and excited to see him, Sally wanted to chide him never to sneak up on her like that.

But when she parted her lips to speak, Taign's mouth hungrily claimed hers.

She swallowed back a soft cry and let any memories of broken promises fade away. She had Taign in her arms. And wasn't that the only thing she'd ever truly wanted?

Taign resolutely claimed Sally in a kiss and she responded willingly. He never meant to shake her up in doing so, but he needed to be near her once again—he simply couldn't help himself. He'd already learned what it was like to be in her life, and he hadn't been able to think of anything else since.

He broke their kiss and nestled his lips into her soft hair. "Sally, you make me crazy inside. I tried to be all business, but I can't. Not when it comes to you. It tears me up. You make me do things I can't help, like wanting to save this place, no matter what the numbers tell me. I'm sorry. Can you forgive me for not believing in you?" he asked between hardened, labored breaths.

"No, don't you dare apologize. Not for anything. No apologies."

He felt her pull away and inspect his gaze. She blinked away a swollen tear that clung to the rim of her eye. The innocence in her gaze matched the same innocent, wide-eyed expression he'd always remembered.

"I've been so hard on you, and I tried to force you back to New York, but you wouldn't budge. You wouldn't leave me," she whispered.

"I don't ever want to leave you," he told her honestly, hopeful he'd finally gained her trust. But her trust was something he'd probably never feel worthy of.

"I believe you. And trust you," she blurted out.

"It's about time!" He let out a low laugh. He loved hearing those words. In fact, he loved everything about her, right down to her heart and soul. He always had. Overpowered by feelings of love he'd never experienced until now, Taign clung to her. "I'll never leave you. Never want to let you go. You have my word."

With her still in his embrace, he walked her back up to the main house and didn't let go of her for the rest of the evening, not for a moment.

Something woke Sally from her sleep, but she immediately recognized it for what it was: her own noisy incessant thoughts. She lifted her head from the pillow and peered over at the window. Somewhere out there, somewhere amid the meadowlands, Taign was camping out alone in a bog house.

Could he be awake too, thinking about her as she was thinking about him?

Accosted by recollections of the day, especially his last kiss, she smiled. Broadly. Together, they'd shared a dinner with all the men, their wives, and oodles of kids. By the time she'd fallen into bed, happily exhausted by the day's labor, she had finally convinced herself that having Taign in her life for good was real.

But so were the problems they faced.

While Sally had to face the inevitable loss of Misty Meadows, Taign stood to lose so much more. Especially if he hung around, seeing this harvest through to its bitter end. Not only would he share in the loss of the bogs, but also the loss of his livelihood. She already knew she couldn't allow it to happen. He'd worked so hard and come so far, she couldn't let him throw it all away for her.

He'd worked ceaselessly to make things right with her.

Now it was her turn.

With sudden determination, she left the warmth of her bed. The brisk night air played against her skin as she changed into jeans and a sweatshirt. After tugging on thick socks to protect her feet from the cold hardwood floor, she padded out of the room and down the stairs.

She approached the computer station and rummaged through the pile of papers until she came to the document in question.

The Letter of Intent to sell off part of Misty Meadows.

She took a moment to quickly peruse the legal jargon before her gaze fell on the blank signature line. The time had come to put her faith in Taign's decision to sell his share. The time had come to let the bogs go. If she didn't let him sell, he'd lose everything. He'd lost enough as it was.

To think she'd spent the better part of these past couple of weeks trying to get Taign out of her life. He'd spent just as much time convincing her he wouldn't leave her again. And now that she readily accepted his decision to stay and was glad to have him in her life again, she now had to set him free. Letting him go was the last thing she wanted to do, yet it was the biggest sacrifice she could make.

She could no longer hang onto a dream and allow Taign's hard-earned future success slip through his fingers. She willed herself to be strong and started to reach for the pen.

"Sally?"

Sally halted to look at the doorway at the other end of the living room. The only source of light came from a small night-light in the kitchen. Silhouetted by the minimal light source, Taign's hardened, lean form was unmistakable in the surrounding darkness. What would she do without him in her life?

"Taign? What are you doing here?"

"Couldn't sleep. So I just made the rounds, checking on the sprinklers. I figured I wouldn't be going back to bed anytime soon, so I stopped in for a minute to get warm on the way back to the bog house."

"I didn't even hear you come in."

"It's after midnight. Have you even been to bed?"

"Yeah, but I couldn't sleep either," she began, "I've got too much on my mind." Her gaze returned to the document in her grasp.

He stepped out of the faint illumination from the night-light, and crossed the living room, all the while pointing at the document in her hand. "What are you doing with the Letter of Intent?"

"I'm signing it. I know what you're up to and I won't let you do it."

"What do you mean? Let me do what?"

"I can't let you throw away everything you've worked so hard for in New York. Like your career. There's no sense in us both losing everything."

"Sal, I know you don't want to sign it. For Pete's sake, don't sign it on account of me."

But his words didn't stop her. She reached for the pen on the desk, until he leaned over and swiped the pen from her.

"You were right all along," she asserted. "I've been holding onto a pipe dream. We can't even get through this one harvest—"

"How'd you find that out?"

"Doesn't matter. It's about time I face reality. If I care so much about this place, then it's time to give it a real chance with someone who can run it right. Now give me back the pen. I can't let you throw away your future. I can't let you lose everything you worked so hard for." She tried to hide the tears in her voice. "I've got to send you back to New York."

"I'd like to see you try."

Even in the dark, she could see his eyes narrow in proud determination. When he stood tall in his refusal, she said, "Fine. I'll get a pen from the kitchen."

With letter in hand, she spun on her heel and proceeded to the next room. She'd barely made it to the dimly lit kitchen and opened a drawer when Taign came up behind her. He briskly closed the drawer, almost pinching her fingers in the process.

"What are you doing?" she demanded.

"I'm stopping you from doing something you'll regret. Now give me the letter."

"Don't you see? You were right."

"And I'm telling you I'm wrong." He placed his muscled body in front of the drawer to keep her from getting another pen.

"You're going back to New York for good. You have to." Her throat burned and she willed herself not to cry. She couldn't let him do it—simply throw away what was so important to him. To prevent it, she was willing to sacrifice the bogs—and sacrifice her love for him—to see that he didn't lose any more of what life had to offer him.

He tugged the papers out of her hand. "I'm locking these in the desk drawer; don't bother looking for the key." He disappeared from the kitchen and walked into the living room. "We'll find some other way."

"Taign! Why are you so—"

A movement suddenly caught the corner of her eye, and Sally stopped her words. She peered out through the kitchen's large bay window overlooking the bogs. She saw it again. A flicker of a flashlight, maybe. It shut off, then on, then off again. Someone was lurking amid the equipment out by the bogs.

Sally's thoughts narrowed. As if experiencing tunnel vision, she didn't think twice about putting a stop to the perpetrator. With a mounting anger at whoever was out there tampering with the equipment, she slipped her toes into the work boots she'd left at the door earlier. Taign would simply have to catch up. She had to get to the bottom of things *now*. It could be too late if she waited for him.

Shrugging on her jacket, she called out, "Meet me outside!"

"What's going on?" he called back from the other room.

In too much of a hurry to answer, she anxiously grabbed the flashlight from the wall. As she stormed out the door she heard him say, "Don't go out without me! You don't know what's out there!"

Too late to worry about that now. The source of her trouble could possibly be causing more problems outside, and she couldn't let it happen. She kept the flashlight off, and with a quiet anger, she hurried down the small hill toward the flooded bog. A surprise attack on the intruder would give her the advantage, and Taign's arrival would be her secret weapon.

She kept her gaze on the general area where she'd first seen the light, but all remained in shadow under the thick blanket of clouds. While the black of night made it tough to pinpoint the culprit, she knew the darkness also aided her in her surprise attack. She knew he had to be there somewhere.

The flash of light appeared again, then disappeared.

The flash allowed her the chance to zero in on her target. As she approached the large trailer truck still parked along the edge of the flooded bog, the tall cranberry elevator towering over the truck came into view.

And so did the intruder.

Sally's heart thudded, her chest constricted. She looked back in search of Taign.

Nothing.

She had to think with her head, and not act on emotion. She hid behind the truck and remained out of view.

She waited.

And watched.

The dark figure slowly skulked back and forth beside the truck, paused to turn on a flashlight, then closely inspected the controls to the cranberry elevator and belt. The heavyset figure then started to tinker with the mechanical controls, until the flashlight flickered out. The perpetrator shook the flashlight, bringing it to light once again, and continued tinkering.

Sally's heart lurched in her throat. She couldn't let whoever it was sabotage this crucial piece of equipment, not when it could endanger the lives of those who operated it. And certainly not when their whole harvest depended on it.

She had barely finished her thoughts when a faint alarm sounded in the main house.

A sense of dread filled her. The alarm indicated that the temperature was dipping to freezing, which would lead to killer frost. A potentially dangerous intruder was bad enough, but now she had an entire crop to protect and sprinklers to start up. She needed to stop the stranger, but she also knew she had to get down to the pump house soon to fire up the gas-powered motors. Starting the motor to set the sprinklers in motion would do her no good, however, if it meant this stranger still had free access to the equipment. She had to stop him and see who it was before the noisy alarm drove him away. Quickly, she turned her flashlight on the trespasser.

"Stop right there!" she yelled and set her sights on the perpetrator. As she recognized the person, however, she had to blink twice. She couldn't rely on her own eyes in the dark of the night; couldn't believe the one person she had trusted could be the one person responsible for all of her problems.

Chapter Thirteen

"Casso?"

Sally's flashlight illuminated the heavy set older man. Startled, he squinted into the beam of brightness before he stumbled back in shock. As the man helplessly started to fall, Sally's heart sank.

Casso tried to keep his balance by grabbing on to the side of the cranberry elevator, but he missed. Sally dropped the flashlight and ran forward to help the tumbling old man.

"It was the only way!" he cried out into the darkness. "I had to keep him here as long as possible!"

"Who?"

"Taign!"

Casso landed hard against the antiquated machinery. To break his fall, he braced himself against the controls, which sent the conveyor belt rumbling upward into the truck. In the dark of night, Sally fumbled to help steady Casso, who then toppled to the ground. He clutched at his chest and started breathing hard. Too hard.

"Casso!" she cried out while she grabbed his beefy arm.

"Taign belongs here," he said between hefty breaths, "he needs to see that. So do you."

"So you messed around with the equipment to get him to stay and help? How could you?" she demanded, horrified he'd do such a thing.

"I did it for your dad. And for me too—"

"What do you mean?"

"—but things went too far . . . the Letter of Intent," he said, lightly gasping now, "I couldn't let that happen to me."

"Let what happen to you?" Sally asked, impatient for an answer. With one last effort, she tried to help Casso get to his feet, but as he rose, he stumbled once more.

She leaned over to grab him when suddenly something caught onto her, and tugged her along. Somehow, her jacket had gotten snagged in the cranberry elevator's conveyor belt and chain. She had no choice but to leave Casso on the ground. Quickly, she focused on her entanglement with the rising belt.

The jacket quickly tightened about her, which made it impossible to escape. Her arm twisted in an unnatural position, and she cried out as her feet left the ground. With her legs dangling in the air, she knew she was headed upward. Panic gripped her as she became weightless, at the mercy of the conveyor belt and chain. With her last ounce of energy, she desperately fought to cling to the machinery, hoping to gain her balance as she ventured upward into the darkness of the night. She hung on, still attempting to break from her snagged jacket, despite the pain in her arm.

She knew one thing. A fall from the elevator at ten

feet in the air was better than going over the top of the belt like a roller coaster ride at twenty feet. She couldn't plummet from so high, down into the truck. Doing so could mean death.

Amid the noisy hum of the machine, Sally heard Taign's shouts. She thought she'd heard the words "hang on," but couldn't be sure—she was too busy trying to unzip her jacket somehow and struggle loose from the equipment.

Almost free from the jacket, she heard a sharp thud of the machine's controls, followed by the halt of the conveyor belt. The sudden jolt was just enough for her to free herself once and for all. But when she did, she lost her grip and plummeted into blackness.

It had to have been a dream, Sally thought once she opened her eyes. The first thing she saw was Taign's glorious face. He looked tired—and even a little worried. But he also looked happy.

Trouble was, she wasn't in her own bed. And it wasn't a dream. Taign sat in a chair next to her hospital bed. She forced her achy eyes to look down at her body, to her right arm, set in a cast, strategically adorned with some sort of brace wrapped around her right shoulder. Every inch of her either ached or throbbed.

"Let me guess," she said through the hoarseness of her throat, "a cracked-up collarbone and a broken arm." At least, that's what her pain indicated to her.

He smiled despite his sad eyes. "You guessed two out of three. You also got yourself a fashionable headband around your skull. It's a great look for you," he teased, despite the exhausted hurt in his expression. "Very stylish for someone with a banged-up melon like yours. But it was better than the drowned-rat look you had after you rolled into the water."

"Better than landing inside the truck, I suppose," she said, not quite able to sift through the jumble of broken mental images. She lifted her unbound hand to the bandage on her head. Nope. Definitely not a dream. "What happened?"

"You got caught up in the cranberry elevator chain. You were about halfway up when you took a fall—" His voice quivered in anguish and he looked away. Her heart went out to him. With her good arm, she reached over and laid stiff fingers on his forearm.

He sat perfectly still, as if terrified to return her touch. "You could've snapped your neck like a twig. Got yourself killed. I couldn't stop the elevator in time. Sal, I—I wasn't there for you." He still wouldn't look at her.

"Are you kidding?" She spoke slowly. "Since the day you showed up, you've been there for me. And all you've done is apologize for it. This was my fault. I took off. I should have listened to you." When another cluster of memories formed in her head, she spoke the name, "Casso."

He finally brought his grief-stricken face up to hers. "He's doing all right. He'll be released soon."

"Released?" she whispered.

"Had himself an angina attack. He got pretty worked up over the whole thing. I don't think he could feel any more rotten."

"I wish I could remember what happened."

"It'll probably come to you in time, but I'm no expert in these things. As for Casso, I'll give you the short version. He was the one helping the neglect along."

"But why?"

"He knew how important it was to your dad to get us together to save Misty Meadows. But even more so, Casso didn't want to lose his home any more than you did. It's the only real home he's known and he was terrified it would be taken away from him. So, he made problems, hoping if word got out that the bogs were a bad investment, then no one would buy the place. When he discovered the Letter of Intent, he got desperate. He felt he had to do something drastic to get John to bow out."

Sally closed her eyes. She tried to make sense of the old man's actions. But concentrating on it only made her head throb.

"So, Casso was trying to see my father's last wishes through? To see us turn Misty Meadows around? And keep his home in the process?"

"He knew the value of the property was dwindling. The old guy feared he'd eventually have no place to go if the place got sold. I guess he felt if anyone could salvage the damages, we could. As for your dad, I'm sure he didn't know just how bad things got before he died."

"But my dad did know I was off pursuing another career at the time," she told him.

"And somehow he knew you'd come home. He knew you and I together wouldn't let him down."

"But I still can't believe Casso made so much trouble."

"Well, he didn't mean to let things get so out of control. In fact, when you caught him, he was actually trying to fix some of the damages he'd done."

"Seems we've all been trying to fix the damages we've created for ourselves," Sally whispered.

She felt Taign's warm hand cover her own, followed by a soul-reaching kiss to her lips. She gazed at him with wonder. Taign had become her world. And she liked it that way.

"Sal, I have to ask," he began, but stopped long enough to kiss the soft inside of her wrist. "Are we . . . together?"

Oh, you crazy fool, she wanted to say. But it would have hurt too much to lecture him.

"You can't give up everything for me."

"To me, you *are* everything. And I won't give you up."

She opened her mouth, ready to tell him he didn't know what he was saying. But no words came. It hurt too much to try and make him leave. And truth be known, she didn't want him to go.

"Before you try and get rid of me again, let me say this," he began, "I love Misty Meadows. I do want to save it. We do have alternatives, if you'll consider them."

"I've been so stubborn. I didn't realize I was doing more harm than good. But I'm listening now."

"I talked to Faith more about your workshop ideas and using the barn's loft. They're great options. As for the bogs, you can rent out the land. Or you could go co-op. The bogs can still be yours, but without the worries. Then you can pursue those other interests."

She smiled up at him. "I'm still listening."

"I know you never saw these as options before because it meant you wouldn't be independent, which was your goal, and for good reason. And if you go for my ideas, it would mean you'll have to depend on a whole heck of a lot of people, something you swore you'd never do. But you're ready, Sally. You've been ready for quite some time. Either way, it means we'll both stay here on the bogs. Then no one will be able to take the place away from you. Misty Meadows will always be yours."

"What about New York?"

"I guess that's up to you. If you're willing to go with one of these ideas and pursue your newest adventures, I've got a feeling you'll keep me way too busy to ever make it back to New York."

She opened her mouth to speak, but he placed two fingers over her lips. "There's no sense fighting it—you're stuck with me. I love you, Sally. Plain and simple. I've always loved you."

"And I've never stopped loving you." She'd let the words fill her heart and tumble out. Taign pressed his lips against her forearm; which sent torturous pulses through her.

"So? I have to ask again. Are we together?"

She didn't even have to think about her answer.

"Yes. And if I didn't hurt so bad, I'd jump up and hold onto you right now to prove it."

"Maybe I could help there." He lowered his body against hers, and she inhaled the scent of his freshly scrubbed skin. He nuzzled into her ear. "Love me forever, Sally. Promise you'll marry me. Make a decent man of me once and for all."

"Yes," she whispered back. She wrapped her good arm around his lean torso. "And this time, Taign McClory, I won't let you go."